Making Rounds

Justin looked Elise in the eye. "You know, you really should think about volunteering at the hospital — like me."

Elise felt nervous and happy at the same time. "I already have," she admitted.

"No kidding! That's great! What do you say we make rounds together?" Justin placed a hand on the wall above hers. "It'll be more fun that way."

Justin looked at Elise. He was smiling at her — a nice, warm smile that Elise was getting more and more accustomed to.

"You're on," she said, almost in a whisper.

COUPLES

Books from Scholastic
in the **Couples** series:

#1 *Change of Hearts*
#2 *Fire and Ice*
#3 *Alone, Together*
#4 *Made for Each Other*
#5 *Moving Too Fast*
#6 *Crazy Love*
#7 *Sworn Enemies*
#8 *Making Promises*
#9 *Broken Hearts*
#10 *Secrets*
#11 *More Than Friends*
#12 *Bad Love*
#13 *Changing Partners*
#14 *Picture Perfect*
#15 *Coming on Strong*
#16 *Sweethearts*
#17 *Dance with Me*
#18 *Kiss and Run*
#19 *Show Some Emotion*
#20 *No Contest*
#21 *Teacher's Pet*
#22 *Slow Dancing*
#23 *Bye Bye Love*
#24 *Something New*
#25 *Love Exchange*
#26 *Head Over Heels*
#27 *Sweet and Sour*

Couples Special Editions
Summer Heat!
Be Mine!
Beach Party!

Coming soon . . .
#28 *Lovestruck*

COUPLES

SWEET AND SOUR

M.E. Cooper

SCHOLASTIC INC.
New York Toronto London Auckland Sydney

ISBN 0-590-40797-X

12 11 10 9 8 7 6 5 4 3 2 1   7 8 9/8 0 1 2/9

Printed in the U.S.A.   01

First Scholastic printing, November 1987

SWEET AND SOUR

Chapter
1

Whack! Elise Hammond slammed her locker shut and leaned her forehead against its cool, gray door. Closing her eyes, she took a couple of deep breaths. In the past it had always helped her calm down, but for some reason it wasn't working today. She felt as if she were standing on one side of a painted line, while everyone else was standing on the other.

With a big sigh, she forced herself to stand up straight and stop leaning against her locker door. Elise thought she knew why she was feeling so out of focus. The same thing had happened to her the last few times she'd been between projects: It was terrible having nothing to do! Now, all of her friends were busy, and Elise was bored silly. She wasn't involved in a worthwhile project like trying to save the whales or feed the starving, and she had no idea what to do with her free time.

It wouldn't be so bad if she had someone to hang out with now, like Ben. But having a boyfriend didn't necessarily mean being together all the time — especially if he had his own obsession, which Ben did. Science was his life, and if he wasn't busy tinkering with a new invention, he usually had his nose buried in a scientific manual.

Elise's soft face creased into a frown. She and Ben seemed to be spending so little time together lately. And when they did go out on Friday or Saturday night, all Ben ever talked about were sound frequencies. As far as Elise was concerned, he might as well have been speaking Swahili. She wasn't into physics. In fact, she wasn't into science — period. It had been her worst subject, and she was lucky she had managed to squeak by in chemistry last year.

Elise slipped her arms into the sleeves of her burgundy bomber jacket and pulled the coat over her shoulders.

"Hey, Elise! Love your jacket!" A playful voice echoed through the halls. Elise didn't have to look up to know it was Fiona Stone. Her distinct British accent gave her away.

"Fiona, hi! You headed for the sub shop by any chance?" Elise asked hopefully. "If you are, I'll walk over with you." She gave a quick spin to her combination lock and crossed over to where Fiona stood unzipping a large book bag. Her naturally slim body was covered by an oversized green sweater, and a wide yellow headband held her wavy blonde hair off her face.

"Sorry. Not today. I've got a dance class at four-thirty." Fiona pulled a pair of ballet slippers from her locker and stuffed them into her bag.

"Right. I forgot." Elise nodded solemnly. Fiona had been moved into a more advanced ballet class after the director of her school saw her dance the lead in *Coppelia*. Now it seemed as though all her free time was taken up with ballet classes and recitals. "How do you manage to keep up with your schoolwork?"

"Sometimes it's tough," Fiona answered honestly. "Like when I have two tests on the same day. I usually wind up studying half the night, and then I'm a basket case for the next twenty-four hours."

"I can imagine!" Elise rolled her large brown eyes expressively.

Fiona laughed. "Hey! Don't get me wrong. I'm not complaining. I'd give up sleeping altogether before I'd give up dancing." She reached into her locker for her denim jacket, and as she was putting it on, she tilted her head and smiled. "So, how's Ben? I haven't seen him around lately."

"Oh, he's okay. He's been busy working on a project for the New York Science Fair."

Fiona nodded sympathetically. "Tell me about it! Ever since Jonathan got reelected student activities director, he's been so caught up in meetings I hardly ever see him."

"It does get to be a drag sometimes, doesn't it?"

"You aren't kidding! If I didn't have my ballet, I'd go crazy. But usually I'm so busy I don't have time to miss him."

A feeling of envy flooded over Elise, and she quickly looked down at her sneakers. She knew that if she were as busy as Fiona, and doing something really special, she wouldn't be feeling so distracted and confused right now.

"Well, I've got to go, or I'm going to miss my bus." Fiona zipped up her book bag and swung it over her shoulder. "Say 'hi' to everyone for me at the sub shop, okay?"

"Okay. See you later!" Elise called. She watched Fiona race off, then turned and started walking in the opposite direction. She didn't know where she was headed, but she did know she felt very lonely.

As she walked down the hall, she ran her hand along the row of lockers, tapping each combination lock. Elise was near the physics lab when she began to hear the whirring sound of a motor. She could just imagine Ben's tall, muscular body bent over a synthesizer. Elise knew Ben's science project had something to do with the effects of sound frequencies on human beings in space, even if she didn't really understand what it meant.

She wanted to see Ben — explain to him how she felt, and hope that this time he wouldn't just give her a quick hug and say something about winter coming and suggest she work on finding shelter for the homeless. It annoyed Elise when Ben made light of her confusion: She wanted him to understand and show some sympathy. But as sweet as he was, Ben found it hard to understand her frustration.

She pulled the door open slowly and stepped into the lab. Five or six students were busy working on an assortment of projects. Some wore gloves and white lab coats as they stood pouring elements into test tubes, while others were gathered at the far end of the room, scribbling equations on a blackboard. Ben was the only one who didn't appear absorbed in what he was doing. He was sitting with his chin propped in one hand, nervously tapping his pencil on the desk.

"Hey, Forrest! Looks like you've got company," someone shouted, and Ben turned around quickly, startled to see Elise standing in the doorway. She waved and he stood up to walk over.

"I hope I'm not disturbing you," she said quietly. "I just thought maybe we could go someplace and talk for a few minutes."

Ben shook his head and led her out the door. "I'm sorry, Elise." He reached out and touched her arm. "I can't right now."

"Why not?"

He looked into her eyes and sighed. "I've got to hang around the lab in case the people from the science committee call."

"Oh." Elise tried to hide her disappointment. She knew Ben was waiting to hear whether or not his project had been accepted into the fair. "So you still haven't heard anything?"

"Not yet. And it's driving me crazy." Ben slumped against the wall. "Friday's the deadline."

"Don't worry. You'll hear soon." Elise reached over and put her hand on his arm.

"Yeah, but when? It's already Monday."

"Tomorrow. I bet you hear tomorrow." She squeezed his forearm gently. Elise could tell that

5

Ben was really worried. The sparkle was gone from his eyes, and he didn't seem to be standing as tall as usual.

Ben looked at her and nodded dully. "I hope you're right — "

Suddenly the lab door opened and Dr. Kirsey, the physics teacher, stuck his head out. "Ben, your modulator is acting strange. Better get inside before it breaks down completely." Dr. Kirsey disappeared back inside the lab.

Ben pushed himself away from the wall and shook his head. "Look, how about if I call you later? We can talk then."

Elise shrugged. "Sure. No problem." She turned to go away. Ben was too worried about his science project to have listened to her, anyway.

"Hey," he paused before the door. "I love you."

"Love you, too," Elise said.

"You don't have to make it sound like a jail sentence," Ben laughed.

Elise smiled. "Sorry. My mind's on other things. I'm trying to decide if I should stop by the sub shop on my way home. Think anyone will be there?"

"Beats me." Ben shrugged. "I haven't been there in weeks. But I think Scott Phillips mentioned something about meeting Emily there at four o'clock."

"He did?" Elise's eyes opened wide. She had completely forgotten her best friend would be at the sub shop today. Ever since Emily and her boyfriend, Scott, had decided to enter the Rose Hill half-marathon, they'd been pretty busy training after school six days a week. As a result, Elise

6

hadn't been able to spend a lot of time with her friend. No wonder she'd forgotten Scott and Emily always took Mondays off.

Elise stepped forward, stood on the top of her toes, and kissed Ben good-bye. Elise was so glad Emily would be at the sub shop that she wanted to get there right away. And in two weeks, once the half-marathon was over, Emily wouldn't have to train anymore. They could make plans to hang out together in the afternoon, like they used to.

Two weeks. That wasn't such a long time.

Emily Stevens hurried toward *The Red and the Gold* office, all sorts of thoughts crowding her mind. This afternoon she had found a note in her locker from Karen Davis, the editor of the school newspaper, asking Emily to meet her after school. Finding the note in her locker wasn't so strange — there were always folded-up pieces of notebook paper stuffed into her locker. What was odd was that the notes were usually from students asking for help with their romantic problems, and as far as Emily knew, Karen and her boyfriend Brian Pierson weren't having any.

She slowly opened the door to the newspaper office and peeked in. Karen was seated at her desk, editing an article for the paper. Emily knocked softly.

"Come on in," Karen called. She grinned when she saw it was Emily. "Hi! Grab a seat. Can you hang on a second? I *have* to finish this — sorry to drag you here and then make you wait."

"Oh, no problem." Emily smiled.

"Thanks. Karen turned back to the article and

her smooth, dark-skinned face was once again a picture of concentration.

Emily slid into a chair opposite Karen's desk and looked around the cluttered office. It was small, and stacks of papers and photographs covered the tops of the four desks squeezed into the room. Emily smiled as she saw Karen remove a pencil from behind her ear and make a note on one of the pages of the article. Her fingers were covered with ink from what must have been a recently changed typewriter ribbon.

A few moments later Karen turned over the last page and looked up, her eyes wide with admiration.

"Whew, this is some story. Wait until you read it."

"Will it be in this week's paper?"

"You bet, front page!" Karen answered excitedly.

Emily laughed. "It must really be good."

"Good? It's better than ninety percent of the junk that winds up in the paper! I'm even going to use it as a basis for my editorial."

Emily looked at her curiously. "Really? What's the article about?"

Karen slid the stack of papers to one side of her desk and leaned forward. "Remember Wendy Lewis, who was hit by a car on her way home from school in September?"

Emily nodded. "Sure. At the corner of Rose Hill Avenue and Everett Street."

"Right. Well, this is her first-person account of the accident. She tells how she was riding her bike across Everett Street when a car came zooming up the hill. She didn't see it until she was halfway across, and then it was too late. The car was going so fast it couldn't stop, and the next thing Wendy knew she was lying in a hospital bed."

Emily's brown eyes opened wide. "Wow! It takes courage to write about something so horrible."

"It sure does!" Karen took a big breath. "Wendy's leg was so badly broken in the accident she's still in the hospital. She doesn't ask for sympathy, though, she wants to know why a traffic signal has never been installed at that intersection. She's the second Kennedy student to be hit at that corner in six months."

"I know," Emily frowned. "It's kind of amazing the mayor hasn't done anything about it."

"I agree, it is amazing. It's terrible." Karen glanced over at the article and shook her head. "And I intend to mention that in my editorial. Which reminds me, you must be wondering why I asked you here today."

"Maybe a little," Emily said with a laugh.

Karen sat back in her chair and smiled. "Okay, here it goes. Last year *The Red and the Gold* staff voted to pick up "Candy Hearts' Heartache Hotline" as a regular weekly column, but I never did anything about it because I wasn't too thrilled with the idea. Well, everyone's been on my back about not doing it, and I'm beginning to think that with the right person writing the column, it might be a good addition to the paper after all."

"I agree, but what does that have to do with me?"

Karen laughed. "Well, since there's no way we'd be able to keep Candy Hearts' identity a secret . . . and everyone already comes to you with their romantic problems . . . I sort of thought *you* would be the perfect person to write the 'Candy Hearts Heartache' column."

"Me!" Emily gasped.

Karen leaned forward and propped her chin in her hands. "Yup. What do you say?"

"I don't know. I mean, I'm flattered." Emily tugged nervously at her baggy wool sweater. "But I'm also scared. I've never written for the paper before."

"But will you give it a try?"

"I guess."

Karen grinned. "Terrific! I was really hoping you'd agree." She opened her top desk drawer and pulled out a list of staff members. Emily watched as she wrote her name down next to "Candy Hearts column." "You'll be fabulous, I just know it!" Karen said, slipping the list into her drawer.

Emily blushed. Soon after she transferred to Kennedy, in the middle of her junior year, students began coming to her with their problems. They realized she was a good listener and knew that whatever they told her in confidence would remain that way. But she was still surprised Karen had chosen her to write the weekly advice column. It was one thing to help friends with their problems. It was another to be asked to give advice to the entire student body! She couldn't wait to tell Scott. She knew he would be pleased. Just the other day they had been talking about how let down they would feel once the half-marathon was over. What would they do with so much free time? Scott was planning to work on the sets for the Christmas pageant, but Emily had been undecided — until now.

"Oh, Karen? There's one small problem." Emily bit her bottom lip. "I'm not going to be able to start writing the column for at least two weeks. You see, Scott and I are running in the Rose Hill half-marathon, and I'll be too busy training to do much of anything else."

"No problem," Karen assured her. "I'll need time to promote the column, anyway, and to come up with a way students can submit their problems anonymously."

Emily looked around the office. "How about hanging a Hotline box outside the newspaper office?"

"Great idea. Just like they do for students' submissions to *Imagination*." Karen glanced across the desk. "It'll probably have to be a big box. I'll mention the new column in tomorrow's paper and ask students to start writing in immediately. That way we should have some letters by next Monday. Think you'll be able to stop by after school and check them out?" She stood up to stretch her tall, willowy frame.

"Sure. Scott and I don't train on Mondays."

"Good." Karen walked around her desk. "By the way, did you know that you and Scott are the only two Kennedy students entered in the Rose Hill half-marathon?"

Emily laughed. "Most of the other runners are probably doing the marathon in D.C. in December. There's no way I could handle twenty-six miles yet. So Scott promised to run with me here."

"Well, I'd like to interview the two of you sometime next week. I'll let you know what day as soon as I get my schedule straightened out. It would be great to have an article about it in the paper. Meanwhile, welcome to the staff of *The Red and the Gold*." Karen reached out to shake Emily's hand.

Chapter
2

Elise pushed open the wide double doors and stepped out into the quad. Brightly colored leaves dotted the lawn, their colors shimmering in the shafts of sunlight filtering through the nearly bare branches of the trees. She kicked idly at them, invigorated by the crisp autumn air. She was glad she was going to be spending the afternoon with her best friend.

She scooped up a handful of leaves and tossed them into the air. She was only vaguely aware that someone was calling her name. Then she saw Emily running toward her.

"Em!" Elise cried happily and slung her arm around Emily's shoulder the moment her friend reached her side. "I was just on my way to the sub shop. I knew you would be there and thought we could hang out for a while . . . and maybe talk. You're hardly ever around anymore."

"I know." Emily slipped her arm around Elise's

waist, and they continued across the quad. "I miss hanging out with the crowd. But if I don't train every day, I'll never be able to finish the race."

"What do you mean, finish! After all the training you've put in since June, you're not shooting for first place?" Elise teased.

Emily laughed. "No way! Besides, running a marathon isn't the same as competing in a track meet. There are no medals, and everyone who finishes is a winner, no matter how long it takes them."

"Well, I know it means a lot to you, but I'll be glad when this half-marathon thing is over. I miss having you around."

"Thanks." Emily gave her friend a quick, friendly hug. "But I have a feeling I'm going to be even busier once the half-marathon is over."

"What do you mean?"

Emily dropped her arm from around Elise's waist and halted. "If I tell you something, do you promise not to say a word?"

"Be serious, you know me better than that." Elise rolled her eyes at her friend.

"Okay," Emily said, and the grin she'd been wearing for the past few minutes turned into a robust laugh. She had planned on telling Scott about her new position first, but she couldn't hold it in any longer. "Karen Davis just asked me to write a weekly advice column for *The Red and the Gold*!" she exclaimed.

Elise turned and squinted at Emily as if she hadn't heard her correctly. "You're going to be writing the Candy Hearts column?"

"You got it!" Emily could no longer contain her excitement. "Isn't that fantastic?"

"Sure." Elise looked down at her sneakers and made circles in the grass with her toe. "How soon do you start?"

"I won't be able to do any writing until after the half-marathon, but Karen and I are meeting again next Monday to discuss the details."

Elise looked over toward the athletic field and back down at her sneakers. "Sounds great," she said.

Emily sensed immediately that something was wrong with Elise, and the smile faded from her face. "Hey, are you all right? You look kind of — I don't know. . . ."

Elise sighed. "I'm fine. I'm just a little tired." She lifted her head and looked at Emily. She didn't want to spoil her friend's happiness. If the situation were reversed, she knew Emily would be bubbling over with joy. She was the warmest, most caring person Elise had ever known.

Elise thought back to last summer when she had confided in Emily. They had been lying in the grass, staring up at the stars, when Elise admitted she was no longer sure about her real feelings for Ben. She thought that maybe it was a mistake to get involved with him romantically. After all, their interests were so different, and Ben could be so absentminded sometimes.

Emily had listened patiently, then with a skill only she possessed, she had convinced Elise to give Ben another chance. As usual, it had been good advice, and Elise wasn't sorry she had listened to her friend. But for some reason after hearing about Emily's new job, Elise couldn't bring herself to confide in her about why she was feeling so out of focus. It was crazy, she knew — but she was filled with jealousy.

She took a deep breath and mustered a crooked smile. "It's no big deal. Honest," Elise lied. "I'm just a little out of it today."

Emily gave her a look that implied she didn't believe her. She could tell there was something definitely wrong with Elise. Her friend seemed tense and preoccupied, but she wasn't talking. Emily wanted to give her a little more time before demanding a heart-to-heart.

"So tell me, what does Scott have to say about your writing the advice column? It's going to be a lot of work, and you won't have much time for him."

"Oh, I don't think he'll mind." Emily shrugged as they crossed the street. "Scott's going to be busy designing sets for the Christmas pageant next month, and as soon as he's finished with that, he'll have to start working on his portfolio. He applied to Pratt, for architecture, you know, and he has to show samples of his work at the interview. Besides," she glanced over at Elise, who was walking with her head down and notebook clasped tightly against her chest, "I think we need some space. We've been together almost every day since the summer, training for the half-marathon. Not that it hasn't been great!" she added quickly. "But being that close all the time isn't always good for a relationship."

Elise's head snapped up. "Says who?" she asked. This definitely wasn't what she wanted to hear. She would give *anything* to be with Ben all the time.

"Just because Scott and I are a couple doesn't mean we have to do *everything* together." Emily laughed good-naturedly. "If we did, we'd eventually get on each other's nerves. I like the fact that we're each going to have a part of ourselves that's separate. It'll make the time we do spend together that much more special. It'll give us a chance to really appreciate each other."

"To each her own," Elise mumbled under her breath. She still didn't agree with Emily. One thing was for sure, though: Elise was going to have to find something to interest her before she went crazy.

Chapter
3

"Hey! Elise, Emily, over here!" Jeremy Stone's voice pierced through all the music and noise in the sub shop. As usual, a Bruce Springsteen song was blasting from the juke box near the huge stuffed bear that had become the sub shop mascot.

Emily waved to Jeremy before heading for the counter to place her order, while Elise stood glancing around at the picnic-style tables and benches. The place was just as crowded as always, but she couldn't help noticing that Jeremy and Jonathan Preston were the only members of the crowd seated at their favorite booth. She glanced up at the old motorcycle suspended over the counter without really seeing it. As usual, it looked like everyone else was off doing their own thing.

"I thought you would be out training today," Jeremy said when Emily put her tray down next to his and climbed over the bench. Elise set hers down next to Jonathan on the opposite side of the table.

"Never on Monday!" Emily exclaimed, taking off her sweater and putting it on the bench beside her. "It's our one day off, remember?"

"You mean runners actually take days off like normal people?" Jonathan teased. He held up his Super Salami Sinker Sub to take a bite. The huge sandwich was a favorite among Kennedy students.

"Very funny." Emily screwed up her face.

"Hey, I was only kidding!"

"I know." She glanced up at the antique Pepsi-Cola clock on the wall and frowned. "Have either of you guys seen Scott? He told me to meet him here at four, and it's already twenty minutes past."

"Don't worry," Jonathan said. "He'll turn up sooner or later."

"I know, but there's something I'm just dying to tell him." Her eyes sparkled. "And I don't know how much longer I'll be able to hold it in."

"Now that you mention it, you do look as though you're ready to explode." Jeremy grinned wickedly. "What's up?"

Emily debated for a second. "I can't tell you." She shook her head. "Not until Scott gets here."

"Oh, come on, Emily," he squeezed her shoulder. "That's not fair."

She smiled and took a bite of her sub.

"I'm warning you, Emily. You're asking for it."

Emily leaned over to take a sip of her soda, and as she did, Jeremy reached over and pulled her arm behind her back in a mock wrestling hold. "Ve have vays of making you talk, Miss Stevens," he said in a menacing voice.

"Better let go," Jonathan said, nodding toward the door. All eyes turned to see tall, handsome Scott walking toward them, with a stack of books under one arm, and a long tube containing an architectural sketch in the other. His sandy blond hair fell over his forehead, and the worn collar of his rugby shirt peeked out from beneath his denim jacket.

"You're just in the nick of time, Phillips," Jeremy said, laughing. "Emily was about to lose an arm."

Scott ignored him as he slid onto the bench beside Emily and slunk moodily against the table.

"What's the matter?" Emily placed her hand on his shoulder.

Scott studied his hands for a minute, then shrugged. "I just bumped into Karen Davis in the school parking lot, and she told me she wants to interview us for an article she plans to write for *The Red and the Gold*."

"So?" Emily asked quizically.

"So I don't like the idea of her making such a big deal out of running in a race. It's only a half-marathon."

"Would you listen to him!" Jeremy hooted good-naturedly. "Only a half-marathon. You make it sound like running over thirteen miles is as easy as breathing."

"Maybe not. But running a half-marathon doesn't make us heroes," Scott insisted.

"Speak for yourself, buster," Jonathan piped up. "As far as I'm concerned, anyone who can run more than five miles should have his face plastered on the front page of *The Washington Post*."

Everyone laughed. Jonathan wasn't exactly a jock, and for him, running a half-marathon was about as likely as going to the moon.

"Yeah, but once everyone reads Karen's interview, they'll expect us to finish in record time. You know . . . rah-rah Kennedy, and all that. And if we don't do well, they'll laugh us out of school."

"Come on, Scott. You know you'll do well." Emily slipped her arm through his.

"How can you be so sure?"

"We've been training for six months," she said in her most soothing voice. "Haven't you ever heard that practice makes perfect?"

"Yeah, but is six months enough time? We probably should have started training a year ago."

"We didn't know each other a year ago," Emily reminded him.

"Right," Scott laughed. "I forgot."

Emily looked curiously at him again. She'd never seen Scott so worried. True, he hated being in the limelight, and always chose to remain in the background. But he also never felt the need to impress people. He usually didn't care what other people thought or whether he met their standards. So why go crazy over a little publicity?

"Look," he said, sitting up straight. "Let's forget this whole thing, okay? I'm really not as worried as I sound."

"You sure?" Emily wasn't convinced.

Scott cupped her chin in his palm and tilted

21

her face toward him so that their eyes met. "Positive. Now, Karen said she thought you might have something to tell me." He kissed her lightly on the lips. "Out with it."

Emily smiled in spite of herself. Scott was so irresistible. "Okay." The color in her cheeks brightened. "You ready?" She took a deep breath and blurted, "I'm going to be writing the Candy Hearts advice column for the school newspaper!"

"You are!" Scott's blue-gray eyes widened. "That's great!" He pushed back a stray curl that had worked its way out of Emily's thick mane of hair and kissed her again. "I'm so proud of you. When did all this happen?"

A quick glance around the table told her that Jeremy and Jonathan were also eager to hear her story, so she told them all about her meeting with Karen that afternoon. But as she talked, Emily realized that Elise hadn't said a word since entering the sub shop. Her friend sat hunched over the table, with her head bent and her curly brown hair hiding her face.

"Congratulations!" Jeremy whistled his approval. "You should make a great Candy Hearts."

"I agree." Jonathan winked. "When it comes to helping people with their heartaches, you're the best!"

Emily bit her bottom lip and smiled shyly.

"We'll have to do something to celebrate," Scott smiled. "Any ideas?"

"I know!" Jonathan slapped his hand on the table. "We can celebrate Emily's new column at Fiona's party. It'll be perfect! The whole crowd will be there, and it will give us something to do besides stuff our faces with pasta." He looked around the table, but stopped when he came to Elise. "What do *you* think?" he asked her. "You've been pretty quiet so far."

Elise looked up briefly. "Sure. Great," she said and put her head back down.

Jonathan caught Emily's eye and gave her a confused shrug. It wasn't like Elise to be so out of it. She was a regular chatterbox and rarely kept quiet for more than thirty seconds at a clip.

Emily shrugged back. She'd been so caught up in her own excitement, she'd forgotten how strange her friend had been acting since she told her about the new column. Maybe now was the time for that heart-to-heart, before it got too crowded. But just as Emily reached across the table, Scott nudged her to move over, and when she looked up, she saw Dee and Marc threading their way toward the table.

"Hi, you guys," Dee said excitedly. "Where's the rest of the crowd?"

"Diana's at the dentist," Jeremy replied. "I can't account for the others."

"It's not important. Elise is the one I really wanted to see." She sat down on the edge of the bench and opened her book bag. With great care, she pulled out a stack of photographs and held them out to Elise. "Take a look at these and tell me what you think."

Elise looked up in surprise. The top photograph was a picture of her sitting in a chair, reading to a little girl perched on her lap. The girl's tiny blonde head was cradled against her shoulder, and two big blue eyes looked up at Elise with joy and contentment.

"Just out of the darkroom," Dee smiled. "I finally got around to developing that role of film of you last summer at the Children's Hospital."

Elise turned to the second photo and the third. They were perfectly clear shots of her engaged in various activities with the children — some bedridden, others in wheelchairs. And each photograph captured a look or a tender moment that brought a wave of warmth rushing over her. She remembered her summer job working at the Children's Hospital fondly. It had been the happiest eight weeks of her life. The children had been open and full of laughter even though they were sick, and being with them had given Elise a sense of purpose.

"Well, do you like them?" Dee asked curiously.

"Mmmm." Elise didn't even look up. She went through the stack of photographs several times. They were special, all of them, and she couldn't bring herself to tear her eyes away. Just looking at the photographs brightened her spirits and before long, a smile took over her face.

"I had no idea you were such a good photographer," Elise told Dee when she finally did look up.

"Haven't you seen my photos in *The Red and the Gold*?"

"Sure, but seeing the real photo instead of a newsprint reproduction makes a big difference. And these are different somehow."

Dee nodded excitedly. "Yeah, you know, as

24

soon as I saw the images emerge on the paper, I knew I had captured something special. I mean, just look at the way you're interacting with those little kids. It's great!" She pulled a handful of photographs from the pile and waved them in front of Elise. "It also makes me wonder why you ever stopped volunteering at the hospital."

"What do you mean?"

"Well, these photographs show how much you love working with kids," Dee said matter-of-factly.

Elise stared at her. Suddenly everything was falling into place. How could she have been so blind? It was as obvious as the nose on her face. She *had* loved working with the kids in the hospital. She had stopped because she didn't think she would have enough free time once school started. How could she have been so stupid? She'd been feeling awful lately because she had *too much* free time. She didn't know what to do with herself!

Elise glanced at her wristwatch and noticed it was only four forty-five. If she hurried, she might still catch Dr. Sanford, the director of the Rose Hill Children's Hospital. "I've got to run, guys. See you in school tomorrow. Thanks, Dee!" she said, jumping to her feet. Then she grabbed up her bomber jacket and took off out the door.

Chapter
4

Elise sat down in the soft leather chair opposite Dr. Sanford's desk and quickly explained to him why she was there. She told him how much she had loved working with the children and how much she missed them. Then she asked if she could have her old job back.

Dr. Sanford leaned forward, put his elbows on his desk, and smiled. He was a handsome man with dark hair that had a touch of gray at the temples. He had emerald-green eyes, slightly hidden behind a pair of tortoiseshell glasses.

"You *are* still looking for volunteers, aren't you?" Elise asked, then held her breath waiting for him to answer.

"We're always looking for help. Especially good people like yourself."

"Great!" Elise breathed a sigh of relief. "I can work every day after school, if you need me."

Dr. Sanford laughed.

"And weekends." Elise added quickly.

"Whoa . . . hold on there." He held his hands up in surrender. "It isn't necessary to sacrifice your *entire* life. Aren't there other things you like to do — like play sports?" the doctor asked. "It seems to me that a girl like you would be involved in all kinds of extracurricular activities."

"Oh, I am," Elise assured him. "But right now nothing is happening at school, so I'm pretty free."

"I see." He smiled broadly. "In that case, we'd be glad to have you start out three afternoons a week and every other Saturday. We don't have as extensive a student volunteer program now as we do in summer, so we'll leave your schedule flexible. That way, if something does happen at school, you'll be free to cut back on your days. Does that sound okay?"

"Oh, yes, thank you." Elise was so happy she thought she might cry.

Dr. Sanford pushed his glasses up onto his head and leaned back in his chair. "No, thank *you*," he said, his green eyes gleaming. "Virginia Coggins told me how good you were with the children, and we're delighted to have you back."

A few minutes later, after filling out some forms, Elise was on her way upstairs to pick up her uniform. She felt as if she were walking on air. And for the first time in weeks, she was filled with a real sense of purpose.

She took the steps two at a time, humming to herself, and when she reached the second floor landing, she practically skipped down the hall. The supply room was at the far end, and to get

27

there she had to pass the main ward. Elise listened for the familiar sound of laughter as she neared the large, cheerfully decorated room. As she passed the door, she stopped to look in. The room was filled with children, some playing in small groups, and some on their own. Just seeing them brought a wide grin to her face. Elise now knew for sure that she had done the right thing by coming back to the hospital.

She stepped quietly into the room and stood gazing at the children's faces. None were familiar, which she took as a good sign. It meant that most of her little friends were back home with their families. And while Elise was going to miss them, she was glad they were no longer here.

She smiled as she watched two boys trying to build a space ship out of colored blocks. She was about to ask if they needed any help when she was distracted by a sniffling whimper. Elise turned and saw a little girl, not more than five years old, sitting in a wheelchair. Her left leg was extended, and she just sat there crying.

Elise ran over and knelt down beside her. "What's wrong?"

The little girl rubbed her cheek with the back of her hand and pointed to the floor. "Marabelle's hurt."

Elise leaned over to see what she was talking about and spotted a doll lying facedown on the floor beside the wheelchair.

"Oh, dear. It's a good thing Marabelle is in the hospital," Elise said, reaching out to pick up the doll. "If she's hurt badly, we can make her

28

better. What do you think?" She placed the doll in the little girl's lap. "Is anything broken?"

The little girl sniffled a few more times, then looked at Elise and nodded. "Her leg is hurt. Like mine. And she needs an operation."

Elise glanced at the cast on the girl's left leg, and noticed it went from her toes all the way up to her hip.

"Okay. We can take care of that." She pulled up a nearby chair and sat down. "Why don't you be the doctor, and I'll be your assistant?"

The little girl nodded her blonde head eagerly, but soon she got tired of the game and, instead of smiling, the little girl looked up and scowled.

"Is something wrong?" Elise looked at the doll, and it suddenly occurred to her what was wrong. She jumped up and gently removed the bright yellow ribbon from around the girl's hair. "How's this?" she smiled as she wrapped it around Marabelle's left leg to look like a cast. "Now you're twins!"

The girl grinned eagerly. Elise stood up, and as she took a step backward, she suddenly bumped into someone. "Oh, excuse me!" she exclaimed, and spun around to find herself staring into a pair of deep blue eyes.

"It's my fault, actually," the boy said, reaching a hand out to steady her. "I should have let you know I was standing here. You're very good with children. Can you work some of your magic on my friend Danny over there?" He nodded toward a brown-haired boy sitting at a small table across the room. "He had dialysis today, and he's refusing to eat his dinner."

Elise didn't know what to say. The boy standing in front of her looked to be around her age and had broad shoulders and long legs. His dirty-blond hair framed a boyish face that appeared sensitive and caring. But what made Elise pause were his eyes. They were a beautiful blue, but very sad.

"Well?" the boy asked after a moment of silence.

"Oh, I'm sorry." Elise felt a blush of color in her cheeks. "Sure. I can try."

"Great! I really appreciate it. Come on over and I'll introduce you."

He led Elise to the little boy. "Danny's been in the hospital for weeks. He needs a kidney transplant, but the doctors are having trouble finding a donor, and until they do, Danny has to stay on a dialysis machine."

She sat down on the chair next to Danny and lowered her face to his. "Hi." She smiled. "I hear you're waiting for a brand-new kidney."

Danny nodded. "I only have one. And it's no good."

"I see." Elise leaned an elbow on one knee and rested her chin in her hand. "How is a new kidney going to help you?"

"It's going to make me all better."

"Well, you're going to have to take care of this new kidney, you know," Elise said.

Danny's expression grew thoughtful.

"If I were a kidney, I would want to be fed," she continued softly. "Wouldn't you?"

For a moment there was no response. Then Danny nodded hesitantly.

"Tell you what," Elise said. "Why don't you show me how you're going to feed your new kidney?" She picked up his fork and held it out to him.

Danny took it from her and very slowly lifted a small piece of chicken to his mouth.

"Good for you!" Elise gave him a huge smile. "Let me see you do that again."

After a few minutes Danny was having fun playing the game. "Now, if you finish all your rice, maybe you can have a special dessert," Elise prompted.

Danny grinned. "Chocolate ice cream?"

"Why not! One scoop or two?"

"Two!" Danny nodded his small head eagerly.

Elise reached over to ruffle his golden brown hair. "Okay, we'll see what we can do about that." She turned to the boy still standing beside her and smiled. It felt great to be back at the hospital.

"You really are incredible when it comes to dealing with kids," the boy said, shaking his head in amazement as he and Elise stepped out into the hall.

"Thanks." Elise turned to look at him more closely. He wore a green hospital jacket over a faded blue T-shirt and a pair of old Levi's with a patch on one knee. He was tall, but not as tall as Ben, and when he smiled his whole face lit up. His eyes, however, remained solemn. "Don't forget to bring Danny his ice cream," Elise said.

"I won't." The boy nodded hello to an orderly as he passed them in the hall.

31

"How's it going, Justin?" the orderly called out.

"I guess your name is Justin," Elise smiled.

"Yeah, Justin McMaster." He held out his hand.

"Nice to meet you, Justin. I'm Elise Hammond."

"I know."

"You do?" Elise looked startled. She had never seen this boy before.

"I've seen you around," Justin said shyly.

"You mean you go to Kennedy High?" Elise asked, amazed she'd never noticed him. Kennedy was a large school, but she prided herself in knowing most of her fellow classmates — by sight, at least. "How come we've never been in any classes together?"

"I guess that's because I just started going to Kennedy — since September. I'm a transfer from Stevenson. Gulp, and I'm afraid I'm also a lowly junior."

"Oh." Her eyes narrowed slightly. Elise realized she didn't know as many people as she thought she did — aside from the seniors and the underclassmen that hung out with her crowd.

"Hey, don't make it seem like a crime!" He stuffed his hands into the pockets of his hospital jacket. "I can't help it if I was born in a different town *and* a year later than you were."

Elise laughed softly. "I'm sorry. I didn't mean. . . . I was just surprised, that's all."

Justin started to laugh along with her. "Like I was when you got Danny to eat his chicken?" He stopped and looked her in the eye. "You know, you really should think about volunteering at the hospital — like me."

Elise felt nervous and happy at the same time. It was partially because of what Justin had just said, and partially because of the way he was looking at her. "I already have volunteered," she admitted. "In fact, I was on my way to the supply room to pick up my uniform when I saw the little girl crying in the wheelchair. I start work tomorrow."

"No kidding! That's great!" His eyes continued to hold hers, causing Elise's heart to skip a beat. She didn't know why, but she was suddenly very conscious of his handsome, broad shoulders beneath the hospital jacket, and the tilt of his mouth as it curved into a broad smile. Looking at him made her feel spacy and light-headed, and she leaned against the wall.

"What do you say we make rounds together?" Justin placed a hand on the wall above her shoulder. "It'll be more fun that way."

They were so close that Elise could smell the clean, starched scent of his hospital jacket. "I really should check with Dr. Sanford to make sure it's okay . . ." she said.

"I'm sure it is," he assured her. "Besides, the good doctor has probably gone home already, and tomorrow is his day off."

Elise looked up at Justin. He was smiling at her — a nice, warm but oddly sad smile, that Elise was getting more and more accustomed to.

"In that case, you're on."

Chapter
5

Clutching her book bag with both arms, Elise jumped off the bus and started to jog up the hill. She felt terrific! Even though the hill was pretty steep, she found it impossible to contain herself to a mere walk.

When she got to the top, she leaped over a low hedge bordering the front lawn, and ran up to the white Victorian house. It wasn't a particularly large house, but what it lacked in size, it made up for in charm.

Elise climbed up the wooden steps and knocked on the front door. A moment later it opened a crack, and Emily peeked out.

"Elise!" Emily flung the door wide and practically dragged her friend inside. "Where have you been? I've been calling your house all afternoon, but no one answers!"

"I guess it's a good thing I came by," Elise giggled as Emily pulled her into the hallway.

34

Emily stared at her. "Come on, let's go up to my room." She guided Elise up the wide staircase. Emily's room was a lot like Emily herself, casually comfortable. She had twin beds covered with bright flowered comforters and assorted overstuffed pillows, an antique oak dresser with a matching mirror above it, and a rocking chair filled with dolls. Her desk was under the large bay window, and a yellow shag rug filled the center of the room.

Elise dropped her bookbag onto the floor and flopped down cross-legged on one of the twin beds. She was so excited she could barely keep from laughing out loud.

"All right, Hammond! Out with it!" Emily said as soon as she had shut the door. She sat down on the other bed. "How come you suddenly took off out of the sub shop? Where did you go?"

Elise grabbed up a small square pillow and held it over her face to hide her silly grin. She knew she was acting crazy, but she couldn't help it. It had been a long time since she'd felt this excited and happy to be alive.

She dropped the pillow and looked at Emily, who was watching her intently. "I went to the Children's Hospital to see Dr. Sanford. He's letting me have my job back as a volunteer!" Elise explained enthusiastically. She almost told Emily about meeting Justin, but caught herself at the last second. Not because she intended to keep it a secret, but because she just didn't want her friend to get the wrong idea. Justin wasn't the reason she was gushing with happiness — it was knowing that tomorrow she'd be going back to the hospital.

"Hey, that's great! You're terrific with kids. But why didn't you tell me?" Emily asked. "I was kind of worried when you took off out of the sub shop so suddenly. I mean, you were acting so weird all afternoon and then — "

"Don't remind me," Elise groaned, once again burying her face in the pillow.

"What was it that was bugging you?"

"Nothing, really. Just a temporary case of the blahs." Elise shrugged. She didn't want to get into that now, when she was feeling so happy.

Emily stretched out on her bed and looked up at the ceiling. "Did I ever tell you that you drive me crazy sometimes?"

"Oh," Elise teased. "I thought that's what friends were for."

"Not this friend!" Emily reached out, grabbed one of the pillows off her bed, and threw it at Elise. "That will teach you!"

"Oh, yeah?"

"Yeah!"

Elise sent the pillow zooming back, followed by another, and within minutes several pillows were flying back and forth across the room.

"Missed!" Elise cried out as one sailed past her and landed on the floor.

"I'll get you next time!" Emily replied with a laugh.

They kept up the pillow fight until they were both gasping for air. Then, still giggling, they collapsed on the floor side by side.

"That was fun," Elise said, leaning back against one of the beds.

Emily slung her arm around Elise's shoulder and nodded. "Yeah, but now we've got to clean up this mess."

"Spoilsport!" Elise rolled her eyes and began gathering up the pillows.

As they straightened up the room, Emily asked what Ben had to say about Elise volunteering at the hospital. Was he excited?

Elise paused before bending to pick up another pillow. "I haven't had a chance to tell him," Elise said quickly, not meeting Emily's eye. "It was sort of a spur of the moment thing."

Emily squinted at her. "So I'm the first to know?"

"Yeah. But I'm sure Ben will be glad when I do tell him," she added, trying to convince herself. "Volunteering at the hospital will keep me so busy I won't have time to bug him about staying late at school to work on his science projects."

"If you say so." Emily smiled. "Just don't go falling madly in love with any cute doctors."

"Hi, ready to make the rounds?" Justin asked, walking up to Elise the following afternoon. He was carrying a couple of books, and his hospital jacket was open, revealing a red sweat shirt with the Washington Redskins logo.

Elise nodded and felt her cheeks flush. What was it about this guy that made her so flustered? It didn't make sense. She dropped her eyes and pretended to check the buttons on her white hospital jacket. She already had a boyfriend. Why was Justin affecting her like this? This was like . . . like the way she had felt about Matt Jacobs last summer. Only these feelings were much stronger.

"Come over here a sec. I've got something to show you." Justin took Elise by the arm and guided her over to two seats by the nurses' station. They sat down, shoulders touching, and Justin leaned close to her and held out one of the slim books. "I borrowed these from the hospital library. What do you think?"

Elise's shoulder tingled where it touched his, but she forced herself to ignore her reaction as Justin flipped through the children's book. "Aren't they a little too old for most of the kids?" She wrinkled her forehead. "They won't be able to read them."

"They won't have to," Justin said, looking up. "I plan on holding a story hour."

"Oh." Elise nodded. "Well, in that case, I think they're perfect."

"Good!" Justin tucked the books back under his arm and stood up. "Let's go round up the kids."

With the two of them working together, they soon had all of the children moved into the lounge. Elise helped position kids who were able to sit on the floor in a semicircle around a large chair. Then she sat in the back of the room with those who were confined to wheelchairs.

The minute Justin started to read, the room grew very quiet. Elise could tell right away that he knew just how to hold the children's attention. He would change the tone of his voice each time a different character spoke, and occasionally give a look or a gesture to make them seem even more real. Once, when the book described a girl frightened by a mouse, Justin jumped up out of his chair. That made everyone laugh.

To calm them down, he sat back in his chair, leaned forward with his elbows on his knees, and began reading very softly. Within moments everyone else had settled down, too, and you could hear a pin drop in the room. Elise looked around at the little faces hanging on Justin's every word, and smiled. She was very impressed.

When he finished the story, the children begged him to read another. And for a few more minutes, he was able to help them forget they were in a hospital. What amazed Elise the most was how natural Justin looked, sitting there reading to a bunch of kids. He really seemed to be having fun. And in her eyes, that made him special. She suddenly realized that she wanted very much to get to know him better.

As if reading her mind, when Justin finished the second story, he came over to Elise. "Want to join me for a soda?"

Her heart skipped a beat. "Are you sure it's okay for us to leave the kids? I don't want to get into trouble my first day back."

"It's okay," he assured her. "It's time for the nurses to give the kids their medicine. I always disappear for a few minutes around this time."

"Okay then, a soda sounds good," she said as they headed toward the staircase.

The cafeteria was all the way at the end of the wide main floor corridor, and when they reached the double glass doors, Justin held one open for Elise. Almost immediately the scent of freshly baked apple pie hit them.

"Wow! This sure is my lucky day!" Justin sniffed as he led Elise to the counter. When a cafeteria worker appeared a moment later, he ordered two sodas and a piece of the Special Pie of the Day. "It's my favorite," he explained, after they sat at a table by the window.

Elise propped her elbows on the table, chin in hand. She was determined to appear casual even though she was very excited to be sitting across from Justin. "How long have you been volunteering at the hospital?" she asked innocently. Immediately she sensed it had been the wrong question to ask.

Justin dropped his gaze. His hands, which were resting on the table, clenched into tight, tense fists. For a second, he didn't respond. He just stared at the table. When he finally did look up, Elise saw his eyes were filled with tears.

"Since uh . . . September. I have something to tell you, Elise," he said softly, avoiding her eyes and looking at a point somewhere over her right shoulder. "My brother David died recently. He was hit by a car." Elise instinctively reached out to rest her hand on his.

Justin didn't pull away. He merely leaned back against his chair and continued talking. "We used to come play baseball in Rosemont Park, and we were crossing the street when it happened . . .

last June. We never saw the car coming! Same as Wendy Lewis. She's the girl who was in an accident at the exact same intersection — Everett and Rose Hill Avenue — this past September. Only David wasn't as lucky as Wendy. When he got to the hospital, he was in a coma, and he died two months later without ever regaining consciousness."

Justin broke off suddenly and turned to stare out the window. For a moment Elise thought he might cry. He looked at the table again and took a long drink of soda. "We were twins. After David died I sort of fell apart." His eyes glazed over. "I thought I'd be able to accept it. I mean, he'd been in a coma for so long. But I couldn't. It hurt too much. So I started volunteering at the hospital where David died. I figured if I kept coming back every day, it would eventually help me deal with his death. Plus, I could help other kids who were luckier than David. It really helped me a lot, so when we moved and I changed schools, I started volunteering here." He reached for his fork and began picking at the pie. Elise watched as he cut off a small piece and lifted it to his mouth. Now she understood why his eyes always looked so sad.

No one close to her had died, but Elise remembered how she felt when her sister, Delayne, was rushed to the hospital with appendicitis. Elise was nine at the time, and she was terrified she'd never see her sister again. Luckily everything had turned out all right, and Delayne had come home a week later. But at the time, it had been horrible.

41

Justin cut off another bite of pie and offered it to Elise. She shook her head. "No, thanks."

He pulled his hand back and regarded her guiltily. "Hey, I'm sorry if I bent your ear. I know how uncomfortable people get when I start talking about David."

"Oh, no, I don't mind. Besides, it helps to share your feelings sometimes."

Justin gave a short, harsh laugh. "Tell that to my parents! They refuse to talk about my brother. We moved out of our old house, and they threw away all his stuff. It's almost as if he never existed."

Elise was taken aback. "You mean they never discuss what happened?"

"Nope." Justin shook his head. "David and the accident are a taboo subject in our house."

Elise really felt bad for Justin. She couldn't imagine not being able to talk to her parents about something serious. "That must make it tough on you."

"Yeah. It's been really hard not having anyone to talk to," he admitted, his voice full of feeling. "David was my best friend. I knew kids at Stevenson, but I wasn't real close to them. Anyway, I'm getting used to keeping things inside of me."

"You don't have to, you know. You can always talk to me if you want." She took a final sip of her soda, then pushed the glass away.

Justin looked at her silently for a moment, then smiled. "Where did you learn to listen so well, anyway?" he asked, standing up to leave.

Elise laughed. "Probably from my best friend. She's Kennedy High's 'Dear Abby', and everyone is always coming to her with their problems. I guess some of her skills rubbed off on me."

"Well, 'Dear Elise,' thanks." Justin gently took her arm as she stood up.

Elise could feel herself blushing. "Oh, you're welcome. Anytime, Justin."

Chapter
6

"So, Fiona, what are you serving at the party?" Dee asked as she stirred her cottage cheese and fruit.

It was Friday, and some of the crowd was taking advantage of a freak warm spell by eating lunch in the quad.

"Pasta, of course. What else do you serve at a carbohydrate-loading party?"

Marc looked up from his tuna sandwich. "Sounds good. I love pasta. What kind?"

"I'm not one hundred percent sure yet," Fiona answered. "I still have a few more recipes to test out."

"Oh, nooooo!" came a groan from behind, and Fiona spun around in time to see her brother, Jeremy, fall back on the grass and begin clutching his stomach. He rolled back and forth, pretending to be in severe pain.

"What's wrong with him?" Dee asked.

"You want to know what's wrong?" Jeremy stopped rolling and lifted his head. "I'll tell you. While you guys have been home eating steak and lamb chops for dinner, I've been forced to act as a guinea pig for my sister. Who do you think she's been testing her recipes out on? I've eaten so much pasta this past week, it's coming out of my ears!"

"C'mon, Jeremy. It can't be *that* bad." Marc laughed.

"Want to bet? If I were you, I'd stay away from the carbonara. But I *will* admit that Fiona's marinara sauce is great."

"Is there going to be anything boring and non-fattening?" Elise asked. "*Some* of us are trying to watch our weight." She patted her stomach. "Whoever said hospital food was *all* bad, obviously hasn't tried the apple pie at the Children's Hospital."

"Well, Scott is certainly storing up for the winter," Marc observed, pointing to him sitting against a cherry tree, where he was devouring an overstuffed steak sandwich.

Scott finished chewing and looked up. "Hey, I'm in training, remember?"

"For what, running or eating?" Jeremy laughed good-naturedly.

But Scott didn't join in. Instead he picked up a handful of peanuts and popped them into his mouth. "It just so happens, runners are supposed to stuff themselves with protein a week before a race."

"Wait a minute!" Jeremy looked at Scott

skeptically. "If that's true, why have I been sampling pasta all week? Shouldn't we be planning a protein-loading party instead?"

"No."

"No?"

"The day before a race your supposed to cut out all protein," Scott explained, "and start loading up on carbohydrates."

Jeremy put his hand to his head and started shaking it slowly. "I knew there was a reason I never took up jogging. It's too complicated."

Emily glanced over at Scott from where she sat on the bench. She was surprised that he was taking the training so seriously. Just last week he had told her the only reason he'd agreed to enter the half-marathon was because he liked to run, not because he needed to prove anything.

"Just don't let Ben see what you're eating. He might try to talk you into sharing," Elise joked. "You know what he's like when it comes to food."

"Maybe I should practice my recipes on him, then." Fiona shot Jeremy a quick look. "At least *he* would appreciate it."

"Well, if you want to ask him to be your next subject, here's your chance," Jonathan said and nodded toward the main building.

Elise looked up and saw Ben racing across the quad. In his hand was a piece of paper, which he was waving excitedly over his head. When he neared the spot where the crowd was gathered, she noticed he had a big grin on his face. Whatever was on that paper was obviously good news.

"I did it!" He raced up to Elise, and lifting her off the bench, swung her around in a circle.

"Did what?" she gasped. He put her down and led her a few steps away from the crowd.

"The letter, it came today!" He held it out for her to see. "It's from the science committee. My project's been accepted!"

"Ben, that's terrific! I knew they would accept it!" She hugged him tightly and kissed him quickly on the lips.

"Yeah. I'm so relieved." Ben gave her another big hug.

"Does this mean you get to go to New York?" Elise asked, excitedly.

Ben took a step back and gave her a silly grin. "Sure does! For four whole days."

"Wow! How did you get permission to miss four days of classes?"

Ben stopped. "I'm not going to miss any school. They arrange it that way. I'll be going to New York over the Thanksgiving weekend."

"You will?" Elise looked at him wide-eyed. He had to be kidding. They had made plans *ages* ago. Her parents were going to her father's boss's house for Thanksgiving dinner, and she was planning to cook a special meal for Ben.

"Oh, Elise," he squeezed her arm, and she felt her muscles tense. "I know I promised to spend Thanksgiving with you, but that was before I knew my project was going to be in the fair."

She dropped her eyes and swallowed hard. She was so happy for him, but so disappointed they wouldn't have Thanksgiving together. She didn't know what to say. She sat on the bench that was closest to her and looked at Ben.

"Please try to understand." Ben said, sitting down on the bench beside her. "It's not that I don't want to spend the weekend with you. I do, but I can't *not* go to New York. Everyone is going to be there, and it may be the only chance I'll ever get to meet some of the scientists I've been reading about."

Elise leaned back against the bench and stared up at the sky. It was a brilliant blue with only a few puffy white clouds. She closed her eyes and sighed. She hadn't seen much of Ben lately, and she'd been looking forward to spending the day alone with him — just the two of them. "Can't you leave the day after Thanksgiving? You'll still miss Fiona's party, and the half-marathon, but at least then we'd be able to spend *some* time together."

"Elise, you know how much I love you. There's nothing I'd like more than to spend the day alone with you. But the banquet is on Thanksgiving, and that's when all the 'big shots' are going to be there. I can't help it. I'm sorry."

She pushed her fists into the pockets of her jeans. Much as she tried to be understanding, Elise felt like she wanted to scream. She wiped a tiny tear from her eye and swallowed her hurt. "I know. I'm sorry, too."

"Maybe I could come home early." Ben slipped an arm around Elise's shoulder. We could go somewhere and have a picnic. We can get all bundled up. I'll even eat leftover turkey!"

"How about peanut butter and jelly sandwiches?" Elise said. She forced a small smile.

A sigh of relief escaped from Ben's lips. "Fine with me. I'll even promise not to mention the word science all afternoon." He grinned. "And I won't tell you anything about the fair . . . unless you ask, of course."

"You know I will." Elise let her head fall against his chest and giggled softly. "Even if I find it boring, I'll want to find out if spending the last two months locked up in the physics lab has paid off."

"Are you kidding?" Ben pulled Elise to her feet and hugged her. "It already has paid off. This letter proves it!" He waved it in front of her eyes.

"That just means your project's been accepted. It doesn't say whether it's going to revolutionize the world!"

Ben threw back his head and laughed. "If it does, you'll be the first to know." He bent over to kiss her then, and Elise hugged him fiercely. She hoped that by holding him so close she would be able to close the distance between them.

Later that afternoon, on her way to French class, Elise kicked an empty paper cup that was lying in the middle of the hallway. "I think I'm going to join the science club," she told Emily, who was walking along beside her.

Emily stopped in her tracks, causing a freshman walking behind them to bump into her. "Oops! Sorry," she said to the boy. Then she turned back to Elise. "What? You hate science!" She looked at her friend as if she'd suddenly gone crazy.

"I know." Elise stopped and turned to face Emily. "I only want to join long enough to make a bomb. Then I can blow up Ben's science project."

Emily laughed as she started to walk again. "Now why would you want to do that?" she asked.

"Why do you think? To keep Ben from going to New York!"

Emily shook her head and sighed. "You really are upset about it, aren't you?"

"Wouldn't you be?"

"Yeah, I guess so."

This year Scott was going over to Emily's house for Thanksgiving dinner. Her parents had suggested she invite him, and he had gladly accepted. Needless to say, she was thrilled. Scott was the first boy she had ever cared enough about to want to invite to such an important family dinner.

Elise shook her head. "Now I'm going to spend my Thanksgiving eating turkey with my parents and my father's boss . . . and getting mad at Ben for not being with me!"

"Wait a minute," Emily put a hand on Elise's arm as they rounded the corner. "Why don't you work at the hospital on Thanksgiving? They're bound to be short of help, and since your parents weren't expecting you anyway — "

"Hey! That's not a bad idea," Elise spoke up quickly. "How come I didn't think of that?"

"You probably would have," Emily reasoned, "once you stopped feeling sorry for yourself."

Elise looked at her best friend and shrugged. Then a slow smile spread across her face. Just the other day Justin had mentioned that he would probably be at the hospital on Thanksgiving. Elise wouldn't mind spending the day with him. The more time Elise spent with Justin, the more she liked him. She still felt a little flustered when they were making rounds together, or just sitting and talking, but it wasn't an unpleasant feeling. It just made it hard for her to pretend that Justin wasn't special.

Elise paused a second by the water fountain across from the French room and leaned over to take a drink. When she stood up straight, she saw Justin McMaster weaving his way in and out of the afternoon rush hour in the hallway.

"Hi," he said, stopping in front of her.

"Hi." Elise tried to sound casual, but the sight of him had started her heart beating a little faster.

"Listen, I know you take the bus a lot, but are you driving to the hospital this afternoon by any chance?" he asked awkwardly.

"Uh-huh. You need a lift?"

"If you don't mind?" He looked deep into her eyes.

"N-n-no. Not at all," Elise stammered. Her heart was beating so loudly she thought for sure Emily could hear it. "Why don't you meet me in the parking lot after school?"

"Will do. Thanks." Justin gave Emily a friendly nod before hurrying down the hall.

"Who was that?" Emily whispered the moment Justin was out of earshot.

Elise paused before attempting to cross the hallway. "Justin McMaster." She hoped she was keeping her cool. "He does volunteer work at the hospital, too."

"No kidding! He's gorgeous. How come I've never noticed him around school before?"

"Probably because you only have eyes for Scott." Elise swung open the door and walked into the classroom. "Besides, Justin's a new junior — from Stevenson."

"Is that supposed to make him *less* good-looking?" Emily teased.

"Well, no. But. . . ." Elise stopped when she saw Emily grinning. "Forget it!" She started to giggle self-consciously and slipped into her seat.

Emily sat down at the desk behind her. "You know what?" she leaned forward and whispered into Elise's ear. "I think I'm beginning to understand why you're enjoying your work at the hospital so much more than you did last summer."

Chapter 7

Elise slammed her car door shut and started the engine. She felt light and happy, but a little nervous, the same way she always did when she was with Justin. He was sitting in the seat beside her, fastening his seat belt.

"Thanks for the lift," Justin said as Elise pulled the car onto Rose Hill Avenue. "It sure beats taking the bus."

"You don't have a car?" Elise ventured, glancing at him quickly.

Justin shook his head. "Only on weekends. During the week my mom uses it to get to work."

"What about a bike? It's still quicker than the bus, and if you cut across the athletic field you eliminate the hill on Everett Street."

"Yeah, well . . . I don't ride my bike much anymore." The smile had vanished from Justin's face when she mentioned Everett Street.

Elise stopped for a red light and turned to look at Justin. He was staring out the side window, but it didn't look as if he was admiring the scenery.

They drove in silence for a few minutes, and then Elise reached into the glove compartment for a tape. She slid it into the tape deck and flicked on the stereo. Immediately, the car was flooded with a song from the movie, *Stand By Me*. Elise began tapping one hand lightly on the steering wheel, and when her favorite song, "Lollipop," came on, she started to sing along.

A moment later she heard Justin's voice, a little soft and slightly off-key. Something about the way he was singing revealed a great deal of feeling.

"Not bad," Elise said, once the song had ended. "Not that many people know the words to 'Lollipop.' Fifties music isn't exactly the latest thing around Kennedy."

"Yeah, I know." Justin shrugged. "I've got the album at home."

Elise turned left and up ahead she could see the hospital. "You must play it a lot. I mean, you know all the words."

"I guess." Justin didn't look like he wanted to talk about music — or anything else, for that matter. His eyes were a little glassy, and from what Elise could see, his face was tense with emotion.

Elise pulled the car into the hospital parking lot and turned off the engine. "Justin . . . are you okay?" she asked hesitantly.

He turned away from the window and let his head fall against the back of the seat. "Yeah. Sure. I'm fine," he murmured. But a frown still tugged at the corners of his mouth.

Elise squinted at him. She knew Justin was lying. Something was obviously bothering him. But what? She didn't move to get out of the car, and neither did Justin. He just sat there with his head thrown back against the seat, and a sad, blank look on his face.

Elise regarded him silently, her heart aching. She wanted to say something to help make Justin feel better, but nothing she thought of seemed right. Where was Emily when she needed her?

She reached down to unbuckle her seat belt, but her arm hit the steering wheel by accident and the horn honked, startling both of them. Justin jumped and looked quickly at Elise. She smiled back at him and said, "Justin, I thought I was your friend."

"Huh?" He looked at her strangely. "Of course you are."

"Then why won't you tell me what's wrong?"

"I thought I had." He lifted one knee onto the seat and began toying with the lace on his sneaker. "Oh, Elise," he sighed. "Try to understand. I get a little down sometimes when I think about the fun David and I used to have together. I can't help myself."

"Well, why don't you tell me about it? Like what were some of the things you and David used to do together?" She leaned back against the car door. "Maybe it will help if you talk about it. After all, you said yourself that I was a good listener."

Justin gave her a weak smile that almost broke her heart. "Well, when you played the tape it started me thinking about how David and I used to goof off in front of the mirror. We would pretend we were the guys in the movie *Stand By Me*, and we'd lip-synch to the album." He took a deep breath and closed his eyes. "God, I wish there was some way to bring David back. I miss him so much."

Elise didn't know what to say. She ran a finger along the dashboard. "Justin," she said quietly. "Why don't we surprise the kids and put on a lip-synching show for them this afternoon?"

"A lip-synching show?" he repeated.

"Uh-huh. During the summer, the volunteers always did something special for the kids on Friday afternoons." She popped the tape out of the stereo.

"Look, Elise, can't we do something besides lip-synching?" Justin sounded really annoyed. After a moment he relaxed and slumped back against the seat. "I can't do that, Elise." He gave a sigh full of resignation. "Don't you understand? I just can't lip-synch without David. It'll only bring up painful memories. Now that he's gone — I can't even *think* of singing and being happy."

Elise searched for something to say — something that would make Justin realize it was okay to miss David. But by the same token, he shouldn't let his pain and sorrow stop him from having fun.

"Why does it have to be the same?" she asked gently. "You and David shared a lot of good times together. Hold on to those memories. But also realize that it's time you started to do things without David. You've got to let go."

Justin was silent. His forehead was tense, and

he was fiddling with the leather band on his watch.

"You know the words really well, and the kids will love the surprise," Elise added.

He ran one hand through his thick blond hair. "Okay, okay, I'll give it a try."

"Great!" Elise said brightly and climbed out of the car. Quickly she slipped the tape into her jacket pocket and started up the walk. "Oh, wait." She stopped suddenly and turned to Justin. "How are we going to play the tape?"

He shrugged. "I guess we'll have to borrow a tape deck."

"Do you know anybody at the hospital who has one?"

Justin tilted his head and half closed his eyes. "I'm trying to think. . . . Oh yeah, as a matter of fact, I do." He smiled shyly a moment later. "Wendy Lewis. Do you know her?"

"No, but I read about her accident in the school paper."

"Well, since she's been in the hospital, we've sort of become good friends." He continued up the walk. "In fact, uh, David dated her a couple of times last year. She has a cousin who goes to Stevenson. That's how we met her. I'm sure she'll let us borrow her tape recorder."

"What are we waiting for?" Elise jumped up the hospital steps two at a time.

A few minutes later they walked into Wendy's room and found her sitting up in bed. Elise thought she was pretty rather than cute. She had long sandy brown hair and bright brown eyes.

"Justin!" Wendy cried happily. "Hi! What are

you doing here so early? I haven't even had my therapy yet." She gave him a warm smile before turning to Elise.

"Don't worry, I'll be back again later." Justin returned her smile. "I'd like you to meet Elise Hammond. She's a senior at Kennedy, and also volunteers at the hospital. We need a favor."

"Hi, Elise. Wait a minute." Wendy's brows furrowed as she eyed Elise carefully. "Of course, I remember now. You sang that song, "I Can't Say No," in *Oklahoma!* last year." She turned to Justin, her dark brown eyes shining. "Remember? Oh, I forgot — you weren't at Kennedy yet. She was wearing a wig and it slipped down over her face during a big number! Anyone else would have died of embarrassment, but she handled it like a pro," she laughed brightly, turning to Elise. "What ever possessed you to throw it into the audience?"

"Panic, I think," Elise giggled. "I didn't know what else to do with it."

"Well, it made you the hit of the show," Wendy nodded. "I wish I had the courage to get up and sing in front of an audience."

"And I wish I could write as well as you do," Elise responded quickly. "Your article in *The Red and the Gold* was really great. You made a convincing case for installing a traffic signal at that horrible corner."

"Wendy *has* to write well," Justin teased. "Her father is the publisher of *The Washington Daily*."

"Wow! I'm impressed." Elise said.

Wendy looked a little embarrassed. She leaned back against her pillow and pulled the blankets up under her arms. "So, what's the favor?"

"Well, Elise and I have decided to put on a lip-synching show for the kids this afternoon. We have the tape, but we need a tape player."

"No problem, you can use mine. There's only one condition." She smiled mischievously. "You've got to give me a quick run-through since I won't be able to see the show. I have a physical therapy session in a few minutes."

Elise slipped the tape into Wendy's stereo and turned to Justin. "Let's just wing it and see what happens, okay?" He shrugged and she flicked on the sound.

When the music started, Elise began to mouth the words as if she were actually the one singing. Justin tried to follow suit, but something was missing. She stopped the tape. "Relax a little, you're too stiff."

They tried it again.

"Nope. It isn't working. Watch me." She began mouthing the words and as she did, moved back and forth in time with the music.

"Want to try it now?" She rewound the tape.

Justin was still stiff as a board. "I told you it wouldn't work," he protested. "I can't do it without David."

"There's no such word as *can't*." Elise insisted. "You just aren't trying hard enough."

"I am, too. But my feet won't move the way yours do. I feel the music differently."

Elise looked at him as a thought occurred to her. "Okay. Why don't you show me how you and David used to lip-synch to this song."

Without hesitation, Justin turned on the tape

and began strutting around the room. "Hey, that's good," Elise called. "Keep going and I'll follow you."

"That was great!" Wendy clapped her hands, applauding loudly when they had finished.

Justin bowed, then hugged Elise quickly. "Let's go, before I get cold feet." He picked up the cassette player and grabbed her by the hand.

Clutching hands, Elise and Justin raced down the hall and into the main ward. The moment they entered the brightly lit room, dozens of little faces turned to them, all smiles. Elise gave a wink and asked everyone to gather around in the back of the room. "Justin and I have a surprise for you," she said as he plugged in the tapedeck.

Suddenly an infectious excitement filled the air. The children began to giggle and chatter loudly as they dragged their chairs across the room. Elise helped those who were having difficulty, but when asked, refused to tell the kids what the surprise was.

"You'll have to wait and see." She laughed excitedly.

She looked over at Justin and grinned. Even he was caught up in their excitement, she noticed. Instead of a haunted look, his eyes had a tiny sparkle to them. She walked over and Justin put his arm around her.

"Ready?" he asked, once all the children were settled.

"Ready," Elise nodded.

A moment later voices filled the air, and Elise and Justin began to strut across the floor while lip-synching to the words. Their timing was perfect, and each time the song hit the refrain, "Lollipop, lollipop, oh, lolli, lolli, lolli," and they spun around to strut back, the children burst into gleeful applause. They loved it, and when the last note faded, they begged Elise and Justin to do another song.

Elise messed up once, but if the kids noticed, they didn't seem to care. They were too busy having fun. When one little girl jumped up and began dancing around in circles, Elise took her by the hand and led her to where she and Justin were dancing. Before long a dozen children had joined them, and Elise felt terrific.

She turned to Justin when the song ended, to see his reaction, but he had started to walk away. He was headed toward the door, and a moment later, slipped out of the room. Quickly, Elise ran out after him, and found him leaning against the wall, staring up at the ceiling. She walked up to him, but not sure what she should say, just stood there with her hands in the pockets of her jacket, waiting for him to notice her.

When Justin looked down and spotted her staring at him with a worried frown, he smiled. Not an ordinary smile, but one so warm and full of joy it cut through to her very soul. Elise dropped her eyes self-consciously and leaned one hip against the wall next to him.

She felt awkward and confused, and wished Justin would say something; explain why he had walked out of the ward. But instead of using words, he very slowly began to lower his face toward hers.

Elise watched it come closer and closer. Is this really happening? she thought to herself. Is Justin really going to kiss me? She had to stop him. She was in love with another boy.

She opened her mouth to tell him that, but before she could blurt it out, Justin's lips met hers in a light, gentle kiss that thrilled Elise in a way no kiss ever had before. For one dizzying moment she felt as if she might melt into nothing.

A tight, funny feeling gripped her chest and she broke off, needing to catch her breath. As she did, Justin pulled her toward him and hugged her against his chest. "That was for being special," he whispered into her ear.

Elise gasped and pulled away, her pink cheeks suddenly crimson. "Special?" she said in a tight voice. She hoped Justin couldn't hear the thumping of her heart. "All I did was follow your lead."

"That's not what I meant." He smiled shyly. "I'm talking about what you made me do today. You helped me face something I've been avoiding ever since David died. And I'm grateful. It was great therapy, and I think I had more fun than the kids."

Elise was a little relieved that the kiss was nothing more than a friendly gesture. But she also wanted to hold on to the warm, breathless feeling she still had.

"What do you say we put on a show for the kids again next week?" Justin continued, his eyes twinkling. "We make a pretty good team."

"We do?" Elise swallowed hard. She hadn't felt this mixed up in ages — not since last summer when she got all caught up with Matt Jacobs.

Chapter
8

Emily was pedalling furiously to keep up with Scott. They were headed for Rose Hill Park, but instead of cycling side-by-side as they usually did, Scott had taken the lead and was deftly weaving his bike through the tree-lined streets.

Emily shifted gears and leaned forward over her handlebars as they came to a gently winding hill. The wind whisked around her, fanning her cheeks and making the jacket of her blue and gray jogging suit flap. She tried to ignore it and concentrate on Scott's broad shoulders instead.

He was wearing the jogging suit she had given him for his birthday. It accentuated his tall, lean frame, and the late afternoon sun, piercing through the twisted branches of the trees, reflected off the gray stripe across his back.

She saw him glance over his shoulder to make sure she was still behind him before he turned onto the road that led to the park, and she wondered if he would act normal this afternoon. She knew something was bothering Scott because he'd been acting a little strange all week. Then there was his behavior at lunch today. It wasn't like him to take things so seriously, and it worried her. But she didn't want to say anything; that would make him feel even more weird. Maybe it would all blow over, anyway.

Scott passed through the park entrance and glided to a stop near the water fountain. A moment later, Emily pulled up alongside and climbed off her bike.

"Let's do a quick warm-up, then a couple of splits," he said, bending over to clamp his lock around their bikes.

Emily stared down at his blond head, and sighed in frustration. Ever since Tuesday, all they had been doing during training were splits! And she hated racing full speed ahead for half a mile, then walking, then racing again, then walking. She dropped her head and pressed her hand to her forehead. Maybe now was the time to say something about his behavior. He was driving *her* crazy.

He stood up and started toward the jogging path.

"Scott, wait!" Emily called. She took a deep breath and gathered her courage. "I think we need to talk."

"Can't it wait until later?"

"No. It can't." She rubbed her hands together nervously. "Something is bothering you, and I need to know what it is," she blurted out.

"What do you mean?"

"You've changed."

"I have? How?"

"Well, for starters, you've been acting so competitive about this race ever since last Monday," Emily said. "During training all you want to do are splits to increase your speed."

Scott's face reddened and he shifted his gaze away from her face to stare intently at the jogging path, then his sneakers. "Why didn't you say something sooner?" he asked, after an awkward pause had passed. "You don't have to do splits with me if you don't want to."

"That's not it, Scott, and you know it." Emily sighed heavily. She wanted to snuggle into his arms and forget about the way he'd been acting. But her frustration at not knowing what was going on in his mind wouldn't let her. "It's not just the jogging. It's everything."

Scott stood quietly for a moment. "Okay." He slowly lifted his eyes. "I'll admit something is bothering me, but it's nothing I can't handle."

"Are you sure?" Emily asked, confused.

"Of course I'm sure," Scott stood up straighter. "I'm just a little nervous about the race, that's all. Everyone's making such a big deal about it. First Fiona insists on throwing a party for us. Then Karen wants to interview us for the school paper." He thrust his hands into the pockets of his jogging suit. "After all that fanfare, they're bound to be disappointed if we don't do well."

Emily stared at him in disbelief. "In other words, you're feeling pressured?"

"You bet," Scott said. "Aren't you?"

She pushed her hair back off her forehead. "A

little, I guess. But didn't you tell me once never to take things too seriously?"

"So? What does that have to do with the race?"

"Everything." Emily tapped him on the chest with her finger. "If you'd let yourself relax, you might realize that."

"I can't relax." Scott kicked at a loose pebble on the pavement. "I've tried, but the pressure won't go away."

"Then maybe you should drop out of the race," Emily said very softly. She held her breath waiting for Scott's answer.

"Drop out?" he said increduously. "Are you kidding? That's crazy! I've never run away from anything in my life!"

"I didn't think so. I was just testing." She breathed a sigh of relief.

He gathered her into his arms and, with his fingertips, gently tilted her chin up so her mouth was almost touching his. "That's good, because I've made up my mind. I'm going to keep training as hard as I can. If I'm lucky, I might even break an hour and thirty minutes." He leaned forward and kissed her softly.

"But Scott. . . ."

He began backing off in the direction of the jogging path. "I'll meet you here in, say, twenty minutes. Okay?" he called, then spun around and took off, practically sprinting.

Emily just stood there, watching Scott disappear around the bend. She didn't know whether to scream or burst into tears. Scott had never acted like this before! She was beginning to wish she had never suggested they enter this stupid half-marathon.

Emily didn't feel any different on Monday. She and Scott had argued on and off all weekend. Now she found herself sitting in the cafeteria, wondering where Scott was. It was almost twenty minutes into the lunch period, and most of her friends were already crowded around the table. She scanned the cafeteria once more, but there was still no sign of Scott.

Just then, Jeremy Stone slid into the empty seat next to her. "Hi, Emily. Guess who I just saw running on the school track?"

Her eyes widened. "Scott? But it's Monday. He's not supposed to be training today."

Jeremy shrugged. "Tall. Blond hair. Moves like a bullet. It was Scott, all right."

Emily sighed heavily and slumped back in her seat. She knew she had two choices. She could go over to the track and try to talk some sense into Scott, or stay right where she was, not say anything more, and hope he didn't self-destruct. She loved Scott more than anything in the world, but she knew if he continued to overtrain, he might injure himself. Still, she didn't want to do anything that might lead to a major confrontation. And if she tried to talk to him, she knew he would get upset. Was it worth the risk?

Emily leaned forward and rested her head in her hands. Yes, it was. She loved Scott too much to sit by and let him hurt himself. And besides, she was the only one who knew why he was behaving like such a jerk.

She pushed her chair away from the table and stood up. "See you guys later," she said, as casually as she could, slinging her book bag over one shoulder.

"Want me to come along?" Jeremy asked. "In case you need someone to help you drag him off the track?"

Emily gave his shoulder a friendly pat. "Thanks for the offer, but I think it will be better if I talk to Scott alone."

"Okay. Good luck."

Emily nodded. "Thanks. I need it."

As she approached the track, Emily spotted Scott coming around the far turn. He was doing splits again, and as she watched him sprint down the back stretch, she couldn't help notice that he was breathing hard. His shirt was soaked with sweat and his hair hung limply over his forehead.

"Hey, have you forgotten what day it is?" she called out as he raced past her.

Scott's head jerked around, and he saw Emily standing by the wooden bleachers. "It's Monday, why?" He slowed to a jog and started doubling back. "Am I missing something?"

"No." She picked up a towel and held it out to him. "I just thought we agreed to take Monday off."

"Oh . . . yeah . . . that. Well, I changed my mind." He took the towel from her and began wiping the sweat off his face. "I need all the training I can get."

Emily sat down on the bleachers and motioned

for Scott to sit down beside her. "Scott, you shouldn't be training seven days a week."

He draped the towel around his neck and looked at her. "Why not?"

"Because you have to give your body a chance to rest!"

"Really? Who told you that?"

Emily shook her head. Why was he making this so difficult? She forced herself to remain calm. "No one told me. I read it in a running magazine." She sighed. "This article said that runners should always take one day a week off."

"Since when does some writer know what's best for me?" Scott's eyebrows shot up, the way they did whenever he got angry.

Emily ignored the warning. She had to make Scott understand that he couldn't keep pushing himself. "Come on, Scott." She reached over and took his hand between hers. "Why won't you admit you're running yourself into the ground?"

"Because I don't think I am." He pulled his hand away.

"You don't really mean that."

"Yes, I do."

Emily looked up at the sky, then back at Scott. "But you can't keep pushing yourself like this!" Her eyes pleaded for understanding.

"Shouldn't that be my decision?" His tone was harsh and sarcastic.

"Not if you refuse to admit when you're overdoing it."

Scott sprang up to his feet. "Me? You're the one who's overdoing it!" His expression turned even more angry, and he started pacing back and forth in front of her. "Just because you're going to be writing the advice column for *The Red and the Gold* doesn't mean you can go around telling people what they should and shouldn't do — unless they ask." He stopped and stared down at her. "And I don't remember making any such request!"

For a moment Emily was too stunned to speak. Her mouth fell open, and she stared back at him in disbelief. "Scott . . ." she finally began, her voice trembling, "I didn't . . . you don't understand. I love you. . . . All I'm doing is trying to help."

"If you really mean that, then you'll get off my case," he retorted.

Emily looked up at him, her eyes watering. "All right. If that's the way you want it," she said, getting to her feet. Her cheeks were burning and her heart was pounding like crazy. "Go ahead and mess up your body. What do I care — it's your life."

Scott laughed harshly. "That's a quick turnaround. I could have sworn I heard you say you loved me a minute ago."

"I meant the old Scott." She looked at him thoughtfully. "The one who liked to have fun and didn't care what other people thought. Not the one who's so concerned with winning a race that he's losing his friends and his common sense by training day and night."

Scott yanked the towel around his neck and hurled it onto the bleachers. It landed half on and half off the second row of benches, then slid between the seats. Muttering a curse, he stomped over to retrieve it. "Well, the old Scott is gone," he said, turning back to Emily. "And if you don't like the new me, I suggest you find yourself another boyfriend." With that, he tossed the towel over one shoulder and stormed off toward the locker room.

Emily was stunned. Is this really happening? she thought as she watched Scott disappear into the gym. She hadn't meant for things to get so out of control. It was all her fault, too. She wrapped her arms around herself and let the tears stream down her cheeks. If she had stayed in the cafeteria, she and Scott never would have had a fight. But she was too busy trying to give advice where it wasn't wanted. And now she'd alienated Scott. Some Candy Hearts she was turning out to be!

Chapter 9

The first thing that caught Fiona's eye when she stepped outside after seventh period was Emily sitting on the bleachers with her legs drawn up to her chest and her forehead resting on her knees. A puzzled frown crossed Fiona's delicate features. What was Emily doing sitting out there all by herself? It was cool outside, even though the sun was shining, and there was a crisp breeze blowing across the athletic field.

Fiona gave a little shiver. She suspected something was wrong. Emily looked miserable, and she remembered that when she ran into Elise between classes last period, Elise said Emily hadn't shown up for class.

Fiona walked over to the bleachers and sat down beside Emily. The cold from the wooden bleachers immediately began to seep through her clothing.

"Emily," she said quietly after a moment had

passed. "Are you okay? I mean, it isn't like you to cut classes. Did something happen?"

Emily looked up. Her eyes were dry, but her makeup was streaked, and her face was full of pain. She stared at Fiona without saying anything, then closed her eyes and shook her head.

For a moment Fiona wondered if she had made a mistake by coming over. Maybe Emily wanted to be left alone. She stood up and looked down at her friend, "Do you want me to leave?"

Emily sighed heavily. For the past hour she'd been hoping this had all been a terrible dream, that she would wake up and find Scott sitting next to her with his gorgeous smile and the faint hint of a dimple on his left cheek. But this was no dream. She shook her head dismally as a huge tear rolled down her cheek. She wiped her face with the back of her sleeve. "It's Scott. We had a fight," she said, pressing her fingers against her temple. It seemed like she had the worst headache of her entire life.

Fiona sat back down and put her arm around Emily's shoulder. "Why? What happened?"

"I'm not sure." Emily's voice was so quiet Fiona could hardly hear her. "The race has made him so crazy, he's not the same person anymore." She told Fiona about her disastrous attempt to make Scott see what he was doing to himself. When she was finished, her face was streaked with tears. "I never expected him to react so strongly."

"It sounds to me as though you hit a nerve," Fiona said, reaching into her jacket pocket for a tissue. "You know, he probably only said those things because he knew you were right." She pulled out a small packet of Kleenex and handed one to Emily.

"I wish I could take it all back." Emily wiped the tears off her face. She had never loved anyone as much as she did Scott. And she knew in her heart that he had meant it when he told her to find another boyfriend. It was over. Finished. She shuddered when she thought of the cold, angry way he had looked at her before storming off. "None of this would have happened if I hadn't suggested we enter the half-marathon."

"What do you mean?" Fiona stared at her blankly.

"Don't you see, it's all my fault!" Emily said in a shaky voice.

"Don't do this to yourself, Emily." Fiona jumped up from the bleachers and stood staring down at her. "Boys can sure act like jerks sometimes — especially when it comes to sports, I think. It's as if they can't stand losing any kind of competition. They get crazy about it."

"That's for sure." Emily smiled slightly. "But it still doesn't change anything."

"Maybe not," Fiona admitted. "Look, if you still love Scott — "

"Of course I still love Scott," Emily interrupted. "I'll always love him. It's just that after today, I don't know if I'll ever be able to face him again."

"On a purely selfish note, what about my party?" Fiona asked, smiling.

Emily's shoulders sagged, and she looked down at the ground.

"Well, if you're not going to show up, I'm going to cancel it," Fiona said. "I'm serious."

Emily stared down at her hands, then at Fiona. She didn't know quite what to say. She wasn't sure she could stand being at the same party with Scott. What if she fell apart and made a scene? That would humiliate her *and* Scott — and probably ruin the party. But at the same time, she knew it would be unfair of her to ask Fiona to cancel the party just because she and Scott had had a terrible fight. Fiona had already put in so much work.

She took a deep breath and slowly shook her head. "No, Fiona. I want you to have the party. I'll come. Everyone is really looking forward to it."

"Do you really mean that?"

"Yes," Emily nodded. "Of course I do." Even though it would be almost impossible, she would find the courage to show up at the party and make the best of it while she was there. She owed at least that much to Fiona.

Emily spent most of the eighth period in the bathroom pulling herself together, and when the final bell rang, she went to see Karen Davis. She was hoping that planning out the advice column would help take her mind off Scott. Her heart still ached, but at least there were no more traces of her tears.

She walked into the newspaper office, and Karen immediately jumped up from her desk.

"Emily, hi. I've been waiting for you." She walked over to a nearby table and picked up a cardboard box labeled *Candy Hearts*. "Take a look inside," she said, handing it to Emily. "There must be three dozen letters in here asking for advice."

Emily sat down and opened the box.

"Pretty impressive, huh?" Karen smiled as she watched Emily pull out the first letter.

It was short and she skimmed it quickly. Then, without looking up, she reached for another. This one was written on scented paper that smelled like lilacs — Emily's favorite flower. She held it up to her nose and breathed in deeply. It smelled heavenly, but as soon as she started to read it, a lump began to grow in her throat. The letter was from a freshman girl whose boyfriend had just broken up with her. She steeled herself to read the remaining few lines, but by the end she was almost in tears again. How could she help other people after she'd made such a mess of her own relationship?

She put the letter down and began rubbing her eyes. Emily suddenly felt very worn out.

Karen's brow wrinkled with worry. "You know, you really look beat. Why don't you head on home and get some rest?"

Emily looked up at her and blinked. "But I haven't finished reading all the letters."

"Who cares," Karen responded quickly. "You look really tired."

Emily blushed. "Is it that obvious?"

"Probably not, but I know what it's like to overextend yourself by trying to do too many things at once. Remember when I became editor of *The Red and the Gold?* I was still doing *News-*

notes on WKND, and I didn't want to give that up. I even had my teachers convinced that I could do both. Then one afternoon one of the advisers found me with my head on my desk, fast asleep, when I should have been writing an editorial. We missed our deadline that week because of me." She shrugged sheepishly. "And then Brian insisted I give up one of my jobs before I wound up in the hospital, suffering from exhaustion. So don't feel bad, Emily. Just take it easy. Get some rest, okay?"

Emily pushed her chair back from the desk. "I guess you're right. I'll come back tomorrow to look at the letters." She stood up to leave.

"Sure. And don't forget your interview with Scott during study period!" Karen called as the door closed behind Emily.

Chapter
10

"So, when do you leave for New York?" Elise asked Ben as they threaded their way through the parking lot. She was surprised he had offered to walk her to her car today. He was usually so reluctant to leave the physics lab, even for a few minutes.

"Wednesday," he answered quickly. "Mr. Kirsey's made reservations for us on the eleven o'clock train. And we're going to be staying at the Commodore Hotel."

"Mmm. Sounds nice."

Surprisingly, Elise was no longer upset that Ben was going to New York. In fact, she was sort of glad. It meant she could spend Thanksgiving at the hospital — with Justin. Every time she thought about him, she got a warm, tingly feeling in the pit of her stomach. It was crazy. She was standing here with Ben and all she could think about was Justin.

Her head began to pound, and she reached up to massage her temple. Ben noticed and turned to her with concern in his eyes. "You okay?" he asked.

Elise nodded. How could she tell him what was going on? "I'm fine, really," she said, once they had reached her car.

"Want me to bring you back something special from New York?"

"Huh?" Elise spun around. "When are you going to have time to shop?"

"Wednesday night." He leaned his elbow on the hood of the car and winked. "The guys and I have it all figured out. Since the science fair doesn't officially open until the banquet on Thursday, we're going to spend the evening sightseeing, and maybe hit a couple of stores. If anything's open, that is."

"Oh," Elise said, pulling her car keys out of her jacket pocket. It occurred to her that since the banquet wasn't starting until Thursday evening, if Ben really wanted to, he could have an early Thanksgiving dinner with her and still get to New York on time. For a moment she thought about saying something to him, then she stopped herself.

She opened the car door and tossed her books onto the backseat. One fell down on the floor, so she pushed the seat forward and leaned in to pick it up. As she did, she glanced at her watch. Three-fifteen. Justin would be here any minute now. She straightened and turned back to Ben.

"What time do you have to be at the hospital?" he asked casually, stepping around the car door.

Elise looked at him and shrugged. "Four o'clock, but I like to get there early."

"How's it going?"

"Fine. It's great!" She suddenly wondered if he could sense a change in her. She knew she'd been acting a little distant and that it was all because of her feelings for Justin.

Ben put an arm around Elise and pulled her close. "I want you to know, I'm really glad you decided to go back to work at the hospital. Knowing you have something to keep you busy makes me feel less guilty about going to New York this weekend."

Elise pulled back slightly. She wasn't sure how to take Ben's remark. Is that why Ben had been so happy when she told him about volunteering at the hospital? Because it relieved him of his guilt?

"Hey," Ben interrupted her thoughts. "My modulator's in great shape. It's working perfectly now. Maybe I'll get lucky and actually win an award."

"Good luck." Elise smiled half-heartedly. "You deserve to win."

"Yeah. Thanks," Ben answered, his eyes sparkling. "I'm going to start packing it up as soon as I get back to the lab." He tilted her chin up for a quick kiss. "See you tomorrow, okay?" He spun around and took off toward the main building.

Elise slid into the front seat of her car and rested her head against the steering wheel. Why couldn't Ben be more like Justin? Sure, her boyfriend was sweet and caring, but he never showed that much interest in her work, and it was important to her.

She sat up and slammed her fist against the dashboard. Just then she spotted Justin coming toward the parking lot. There was no mistaking the slope of his shoulders and the way he walked, carrying his strong frame a little sadly, she thought. She wondered if he had seen her kissing Ben, and if he would say anything about it. If he did, she would have to be honest and tell him they were a couple. But if he didn't, she would let it go for now. She saw no reason to tell Justin about Ben — not until she figured out what she felt for both of them.

"Hi! Do you always hang out in parking lots?" Justin joked as he slid into the passenger's seat. He was wearing his favorite Redskins sweat shirt underneath a gray windbreaker.

Elise laughed. "Only when I'm trying to pick up a guy."

"Will I do? There doesn't seem to be anyone else around." Justin grinned mischievously at Elise.

"You'll do just fine," Elise said happily, and started the engine.

Once they were inside the hospital, Justin turned to Elise and said, "I promised Wendy I would watch her in therapy this afternoon. Are you signed up for anything special?"

Elise looked at him, a surprised expression on her face. "No. Why?" she asked.

"I thought you might like to watch, too. She's really doing great, and I'm sure she won't mind. Wendy likes it when she has a cheering section. She says it helps her work harder."

"Well, if you're sure it's okay."

"I'm sure."

"Okay. I'll meet you back here in a sec," Elise said and dashed into the locker room. She quickly pulled on her white volunteer's jacket and was back in the lobby three minutes later.

The physical therapy room was in the basement, and the first thing Elise noticed about it was how quiet it was. The only thing she could hear was soft music piped in over an intercom. The music was soothing, and Elise guessed it was intended to help the patients relax. She knew from her experience working at the hospital that physical therapy could be very grueling.

The room itself was large and filled with all sorts of complicated equipment. Some of it looked like it belonged in a health club: Blue mats were scattered around the floor, and off to one side of the room was a set of parallel bars similar to those used by gymnasts, but the railings on these were only waist high.

Elise and Justin stood inside the doorway and focused their attention on Wendy. She was lying on a long, narrow table, with her face to the ceiling and her legs hanging over the edge. As her therapist counted, she raised and lowered her injured leg. It looked painful, but she didn't give up until she had reached one hundred.

Justin applauded and Wendy looked up. "Hi!"

she cried happily when she saw them. "Have you come to watch me walk?"

"You bet!" He gave her a warm smile.

Elise saw Justin smile and she was surprised to find herself feeling really awkward and out of place. Was she actually feeling jealous? Don't be ridiculous, she told herself. There's nothing between Justin and Wendy.

She looked up and saw Wendy making her way over to the parallel bars. Two other girls there for therapy stopped to watch as she dropped her crutches and gripped the railing with both hands. They really seemed to admire her. Wendy looked like she was determined to walk, and she slowly dragged her injured leg forward. When it didn't support her weight, she expressed a moment of disgust and tried again. Each time, Elise found herself holding her breath. Finally, after about twenty minutes, her therapist told her to take a break.

"I don't know about you guys, but I could sure use something to drink," Wendy called out to Elise and Justin. "Let's go into the next room. There's a soda machine in there." She grabbed her crutches and slipped them under her arms.

"You really are something else," Elise said to Wendy as soon as they sat down. "I don't think I've seen anyone work so hard in my life."

Wendy shrugged happily. "Thanks. It's paid off. Three weeks ago I was still in a wheelchair and couldn't take more than two steps without bursting into tears."

"I don't believe that."

"It's true. Ask Justin," Wendy laughed.

Elise turned to him and he nodded.

"I'm amazed." Elise sat back in her chair. "Is it as painful as it looks?"

"Sure is," Wendy admitted. "But if I want to be home for Thanksgiving, I've got to push myself. I can't think about the pain. The doctors won't let me leave the hospital until I can walk the length of the parallel bars without my leg collapsing."

Elise looked at her in wonder. "Wow! Do you think you'll make it?"

"If she doesn't, she'll be out a free meal at the China Bowl," Justin chimed in. "We made a deal last week."

Wendy giggled. "Talk about incentive! I'll make it. But I'll still have to come back three times a week for therapy, until I can walk without my crutches."

"And how long will that take?" Elise asked.

"A couple of months, probably," Wendy said. "Then I'll be able to ride my bike again, and do all the things I used to. Of course, I'll always have a slight limp," she added and saw Elise frown. "Hey." She quickly reached out to squeeze Elise's arm. "It's no big deal. Really. It might get me out of PE." She began to giggle playfully.

Elise and Justin exchanged looks and started to laugh along with her — they couldn't help themselves. Wendy's positive outlook on life was infectious. Instead of feeling sorry for herself, like a lot of people would, she was able to accept what had happened, and even laugh about it.

"What's the first thing you're going to do when you get home?" Elise asked, once they stopped laughing.

"That's easy. Collect on my bet," Wendy said. "After eating hospital food for eight weeks, I'm dying to eat something *real* — like Chinese food."

Chapter
11

The next afternoon Emily sat in the quad, staring up at the cloudless sky. The bright sun warmed her face, but somehow she would have preferred an icy drizzle. It didn't feel right for the weather to be sunny when she felt cold and gray. It only made her feel worse. The sound of Scott's harsh words before he stormed off toward the locker room kept replaying in her mind. She'd tried to block them out and turn her mind to other things, but it was impossible to think about anything but him. Scott had hurt her terribly and while she was no longer crying all the time, she still dreaded having to face him at the interview.

They were due in *The Red and the Gold* office in ten minutes. It would be their first real encounter since they broke up, and Emily knew it wouldn't be pleasant. When she'd passed Scott in the hallway a few minutes ago, he'd looked away and pretended he hadn't seen her. She'd had to fight to keep herself calm.

She glanced at her watch: barely seven minutes to go. She wished there was a way she could get out of going to the interview, but Karen was counting on her. She'd agreed to show up today during her study period, and if she went to the nurse and asked to be sent home, it would only delay the inevitable. Karen had until the following afternoon to write the article and would probably reschedule the interview right away.

With a sinking heart, Emily leaned forward and buried her head in her arms. She didn't hear anyone coming until Elise tapped her lightly on the shoulder.

"Hi," Elise said softly. "I've been looking all over for you." She let her shoulder bag slide off her arm, then sat down on the bench beside Emily. "We didn't really get a chance to talk last night. I thought you might want to make up for it now. Have you seen Scott at all?" she asked delicately.

Emily drew in a deep breath. "Once in the hallway, but he ignored me."

"Are you sure? Maybe he didn't see you."

Emily considered her words for a moment, then shook her head. "No. It was too obvious."

"Okay, so he's acting like a jerk. That doesn't mean you should give up. You two belong together."

"I don't know about that."

"Come on, Em. Candy Hearts wouldn't approve of your tossing in the towel so quickly,"

Elise said lightly. "She'd tell you to at least give it another try."

In spite of her mood, Emily smiled. She knew Elise was trying to cheer her up, and she appreciated the effort. "Okay," she said after a moment. "Scott and I have an interview with Karen Davis in a few minutes. I'll try and get him to talk to me then."

"Good!" Elise leaned back against the bench with a satisfied nod. "I'm sure it'll work out okay. Everyone has fights now and then. But as soon as they calm down, and see things in their proper perspective, they almost always make up. And that's the best part."

"I hope you're right." More than anything, Emily wanted things to be back to normal between her and Scott. "It was such a dumb argument."

Elise put her arm around Emily. "Aren't they always?"

"Now that you mention it, yes," Emily laughed, and the tense knot in her stomach loosened a little. No matter how rotten a mood Emily was in, Elise could always make her feel better.

She pushed a stray wisp of hair off her forehead and looked at her friend. "Enough about me. How are things at the hospital?" She cocked her head to one side. "Meet any cute doctors yet?"

Elise shook her head with a meek smile. "No. But I love working there. In fact, I took your advice and volunteered to work on Thanksgiving." She didn't think she should mention Justin.

"You did? Super!"

"Yeah. I'm really looking forward to it, too."

"I'm glad. Just don't get so caught up in your work that you miss Fiona's party or the race on Saturday. Even if things don't work out with Scott, they're both still on." Emily said firmly.

Elise laughed. "It'll work out," she consoled Emily. "Don't worry, I'll be there no matter what."

"Promise?"

"Promise."

"Good," Emily said and glanced at her watch. Her voice sank to a whisper as all her calm feelings disappeared. "I'm so nervous." She gripped her bookbag tightly with both hands. "What do I do if Scott refuses to talk to me?"

"Relax. He won't. Everything's going to work out," Elise responded quickly. "But if you want, I'll walk you as far as the library. I've got some research to do."

"Thanks." Emily stood up and straightened out her green jersey skirt. "You're a real pal."

As soon as Emily walked into *The Red and the Gold* office, her heart began to pound. Scott was already sitting at a table, his blond head bent over the latest issue of the school paper. She stared at him for a few seconds. Then she squared her shoulders and headed over to the table, trying her best not to appear nervous.

She had no idea what she was going to say to him. All she knew was that she had to get Scott to talk somehow. It was the only way they could begin to make things right between them again. The silent treatment was only for immature people — that's what Candy Hearts would say.

"Hi," she began softly, once she had reached the table. "Is this seat taken?"

Scott glanced up slowly and his blue-gray eyes fixed on her. But when Emily met his gaze, she shrank back quickly. She had never seen him look so cold.

Scott tilted his chair back on two legs and continued to eye her coolly as if he were sizing her up for a role in a movie. Just when she didn't think she could stand it anymore, he said, "Be my guest." Then he turned back to the newspaper.

So much for trying to talk things out. Emily's heart sank. She was filled with a hollow feeling in her chest as she dropped her bookbag on the floor and sat down at the table.

A moment later, Karen came into the newspaper office. "Hi, Scott, Emily." She smiled. "Be with you in a sec." She pushed her red-rimmed glasses up on her nose and began rummaging through the stack of photos on her desk. When she found what she was looking for, she clipped it to the article she was holding and came around to the table.

"Okay," she said, pulling up a chair. With the air of a seasoned reporter, she took a pencil out from behind her ear and began the interview. "Tell me, why did you two decide to enter the half-marathon?"

Emily looked at Scott, but he ignored her. He certainly was trying hard to ignore everything in the room, thought Emily. She shook her head in disbelief and forced herself to turn back to Karen.

"I guess you could say to test ourselves. You

know, sort of a personal challenge." She answered the question for both of them. "We'd been jogging together all summer, and when I read about the race in the *Rose Hill Bulletin* I figured what the heck, why not give it a try. It'll be my first race."

Karen made a note on her yellow legal pad. "What about you, Scott?" she asked. "Have you ever been in a race before?"

He looked up from his newspaper and arched his eyebrows. "Does it matter?"

"I'm not sure," Karen said, confused by his attitude. She peered at him over the top of her glasses. "But I like to have all the facts before I write an article." She kept her pencil poised, waiting for his answer.

Scott shifted his broad shoulders uncomfortably, and Emily wondered if Karen could sense how reluctant he was to be interviewed. More importantly, did she sense the tension between the two of them? Although news traveled fast around Kennedy High, it was probably too soon for her to have heard about their break-up.

"No, I've never been in a race before," Scott admitted finally. "But I don't think it will affect the outcome. I plan on making a good showing. Maybe even breaking an hour and twenty minutes."

Karen jotted down what he said, but it was obvious something about his answer didn't sit right with her. She glanced back down at her notepad and did a quick calculation. "Are you sure you want me to print the last part of your statement? In order to finish the race in an hour and twenty minutes, you'll have to run six-minute miles for thirteen miles."

Scott folded his arms over his chest and slid down in his seat. "Maybe you had better leave it off the record," he grumbled.

Karen gave a little shrug and continued to ask questions. When the interview was over, she tucked her pencil back behind one ear and thanked them for their time.

"The interview will be in this week's paper," she said as Scott stood up to leave. "Do either of you have any advice for other runners interested in entering a race in the future?" she tossed out as an afterthought.

Emily felt Scott's eyes on her, and she caught her breath. Maybe he was going to put an end to this hostile silence between them. But no sooner had the thought passed through her mind, than his back stiffened with tension and his face turned to stone.

Emily swallowed hard and turned to Karen. "I can't speak for Scott," she said, clenching her hands tightly in her lap. "But I've learned not to give advice to other runners."

Chapter 12

"You sure you're going to be okay?" Elise asked, holding the phone to her ear as she paced back and forth across her room. "I can skip the hospital and have Thanksgiving dinner with you, you know," she told Emily. "I know how miserable you must feel now that Scott won't be there."

Emily didn't say a word.

"Em? You still there?" Elise stopped pacing and listened carefully.

"Yes . . . I'm here." Emily's voice was very quiet. "And you don't have to come over. I'll be fine."

"C'mon, Em. Stop putting me on." She sat down on her bed. "I'm your best friend, remember?"

"How can I forget when you're always reminding me?"

Elise laughed. "If I do, it's only because I care."

It was Thursday, and she knew Emily was still

upset about her fight with Scott. He'd been avoiding her ever since the interview. Elise looked down at her copy of *The Red and the Gold*. She had picked it up on her way out of school, and it was lying face up on her bed. Karen had done a professional job on the interview, as usual. Even the candid photo of Scott and Emily jogging together had come out well. They were smiling at each other as they jogged through the park — obviously the picture had been taken before their fight.

"Look, Elise. I know you care, and I appreciate your concern. Really. I do. But my cousins are coming up from Virginia for Thanksgiving dinner, and I'm sure they'll be able to keep my mind off Scott. Besides, the hospital needs you more than I do."

"Well, okay." Elise flopped back on her bed and stared up at the ceiling. "But I'm not leaving for another half hour, so if you change your mind. . . ."

"Not a chance," Emily said. "I'll see you tomorrow at the party, okay?"

"You bet! 'Bye."

Elise shook her head as she hung up the phone. She loved Emily dearly, but she was glad she didn't want her to come over for Thanksgiving dinner. She was looking forward to seeing Justin too much.

When Elise finally found Justin, he was sitting in the far corner of the cafeteria, holding his head in his hands. Suddenly she wasn't so sure she should go over to him. He looked so incredibly sad. But she'd just gone crazy looking for him after walking into the main ward and finding it filled with families. It hadn't occurred to her that so many parents would be spending Thanksgiving Day at the hospital with their children. She'd searched all the rooms after that, starting with Wendy Lewis's. But Wendy had reached her goal, and she'd already been sent home. She started to patiently weave her way around the tables to get to Justin. When he heard her coming, he looked up.

"You look like you could use a friend," Elise said, slipping into the chair opposite him.

Justin stared at her blankly. It was hard to see him like this, but it didn't bother Elise. It just made her want to be with him more. She had to make whatever it was that was bothering him go away.

"What are you doing here today?" he finally asked.

"I'm volunteering today, remember?" she answered slowly.

"Right." He slapped his hand to his forehead. "I forgot. Well, there's not too much to do." He ran his fingers through his hair, which stuck up at odd angles and made him look even cuter.

Elise looked at him and knit her brow. What was bothering Justin? It was definitely something serious. She reached across the table and touched his arm gently. "What is it, Justin? What's wrong?"

He looked down at the table, and his whole body suddenly sagged. "It's all the families here. Seeing them reminds me of last summer when my parents used to visit David. They used to come every day after work, and every time they were hoping for a miracle." His voice was filled with pain. "Only it never happened. David died without ever saying good-bye."

Elise squeezed his arm tightly. She didn't know what to say. If only there was some place they could go — somewhere far away from the hospital — and all these painful memories.

"Justin, have you had your Thanksgiving dinner yet?" she asked, when he looked back up at her. His deep blue eyes appeared almost black. Justin was so upset he really didn't look like himself. But he still looked great, Elise noticed.

"I had a hot dog," He glanced over at the empty plate on the table.

"Well, I, for one, am starved. What do you say we go out somewhere and have a nice dinner?"

Justin shook his head. "Oh, Elise," he murmured, "I don't think so. I'm feeling pretty low."

"All the more reason," she said. "Let's see." Elise began ticking names of places off on her fingers. "There's the sub shop, Mario's, Sticky Fingers. . . ." She paused. "Maybe we'd better save that one for dessert. They have the best ice cream sundaes. Come on, Justin. We'll treat ourselves to something even better than turkey."

Justin leaned back in his chair and studied her face. "I suppose I could go for a pizza with everything on it," he mused.

"Great! Let's go!" Elise reached out her hands to Justin and pulled him to his feet.

* * *

The Pizza Haven, which had opened last year, was narrow and rectangular, with a counter in the back and a row of Formica-topped tables along each wall. Elise reached down and plucked a mushroom off the pizza. She popped it into her mouth. "Mmm. Not turkey, but not bad." She flashed Justin a grin, and he shifted in his chair.

Elise wished he would smile back. She hadn't seen him smile in such a long time. She played with her fork on the table between bites of pizza and wished she could think of some way to cheer him up — or at least get him to *say* something. Food obviously hadn't done the trick. Then as they were walking out of the restaurant, Elise had an idea.

"Now I'm going to show you one of my favorite places in the world." She grabbed Justin by the arm and led him down a narrow tree-lined street into Rosemont Park. It was smaller than Rose Hill Park across town, where Emily and Scott always jogged. Elise thought it was much prettier. It was an old estate, and it had been deeded to the town many years ago. Classic stone pillars stood at the entranceway.

"I haven't been here in a while. This has to be the most beautiful place in Rose Hill." She sighed and looked at the sunlight filtering through the twisted branches of what was a beautiful rose garden in the spring and summer. Even in November there was something charming and romantic about the park. "What do you think?" she asked, wandering over toward the small goldfish pond that was covered with fallen leaves.

Justin stood a few feet away from her, leaning

against an old maple tree. One foot was resting against the rough bark. "It *is* beautiful, he said softly, and it's one of my favorite places in Rose Hill, too. I've been coming here since I was a little boy."

"You *have*?" Elise picked up a small pebble and tossed it into the pond. It skipped twice and made the water ripple. "Boy, you've been in Rose Hill a lot." It was amazing how much she and Justin had in common.

Elise hung her head and stared at a cluster of toadstools on long, slender stems. Why was it that lately she felt as if she and Ben were on two different planets? True, they had shared a lot. They'd been best friends for a long time, and she had many good memories. But now she felt they had grown apart and were almost as different as night and day. She let out a deep breath and wondered what, if anything, she could do to change that. More to the point, did she even want to? Her brow wrinkled into a frown.

Justin walked over to Elise and put his arm around her shoulder. She responded by wrapping her arms around his waist. She didn't know what it was about Justin that made her feel so lightheaded. "What made you think you had an exclusive on the pond?" he said, giving her shoulder an affectionate squeeze.

Elise rested her head against him and shrugged. Other than the sound of a dog barking somewhere off in the distance, it was quiet. Dried leaves were swirling around their feet and the late afternoon sunlight reflected off the pond. Without warning,

Justin began to trace patterns across her back with his hand. His touch sent shivers throughout her body. Elise lifted her head to face him and saw his deep blue eyes already looking at her.

"Elise," he said softly. "I want to thank you for bringing me here today. Being outside really helps sometimes. It reminds me that, no matter what, life goes on. There'll always be another spring." His face was inches away from hers, and she felt his gaze as if it were a physical touch. "You're really very special, do you know that?" He cupped her face in his hands and lowered his mouth to hers.

Elise felt her whole body go limp as he kissed her sweetly and softly. It felt so right, so natural. Her heart began to thump wildly, and her body leaned toward his. Justin smiled for the first time all afternoon. It was such a radiant smile, it made Elise feel like she was floating.

"I've wanted to do that all afternoon," he whispered. "Elise, you've become a very important person in my life. I hope you know that."

"I have?" Elise felt a little dizzy.

Justin reached up and brushed back a stray curl that had fallen onto her forehead. "Do you know what I'm trying to say?"

"Yes! Oh, yes!" she cried, and flung her arms around his neck. She hugged him hard, then relaxed in his arms. They stood there, just holding each other for a while. For the first time in a long time Elise felt really needed. Even though Justin hadn't said he loved her, she was sure he did. And the way she was feeling, Elise knew she loved

Justin back. But where did that leave Ben? She pulled back slightly and rested her head on Justin's chest. Her feelings for Ben had become fuzzy lately, and she suddenly realized she no longer knew what she felt for him. If it was possible to love two people at the same time, she supposed she loved them both.

She and Ben had been friends for years, ever since they were kids. And once they had become a couple, she didn't think anything could ever come between them. If she was to be honest with herself, though, she would have to admit that while she still loved Ben dearly, she was no longer *in* love with him. Justin stepped away and sat cross-legged on a bed of leaves. Elise sat down next to him.

Elise knew that her feelings toward Ben had started to change last summer. She began to realize something was missing from their relationship — the romance was gone. In fact, she and Ben had almost broken up. In retrospect, maybe they should have, thought Elise. But at the time, neither of them had realized what the real problem was: They were a couple whose time together was running out. Elise picked up a stick and traced a pattern in the dirt. Ben hadn't realized it, but he would have to now. Once he stopped to think about the two of them, it would become obvious. Elise would have to talk to him and tell him it was over. It had been over even before she met Justin, she knew that. Elise resolved to tell him as soon as he came back from New York. She couldn't go any further in her relationship with Justin until she did.

* * *

The sun dipped below the treeline and a cool breeze blew across the pond. In a couple of hours it would be dark. Elise leaned back on her hands and let the breeze tumble over her like a wave. It was funny. Now that she had come to terms with how she felt about Ben and Justin, she was so relaxed she felt silly. She picked up a handful of dried leaves and was about to toss them over Justin's head, when he sprang to his feet and began kicking at the leaves.

"Justin?" Elise said. "What are you doing?"

He stopped kicking and shot her a quick look. "I'm okay." He laughed sheepishly. "I just needed to get out some of my anger. I was sitting here thinking about David, and the fact that I'm here and he's not." His eyes were clear and intense, and Elise felt as if she were looking right into his heart.

She wiped the dirt off her hands and got to her feet slowly. "And . . ." she said softly, "you're feeling guilty."

"Was. Past tense." He took a step toward her. "Coming here today with you has made me realize that I've got to go on living. There's a tomorrow out there for me. I've spent enough time mourning David. I have to put yesterday behind." He held out his hand to Elise, and together they started walking out of the park.

"Speaking of tomorrow, do you like pasta?" Elise asked.

"Depends. What kind?"

"All kinds. Fiona Stone is throwing a carbohydrate-loading party for my friends, Emily and

Scott. They're running in the half-marathon on Saturday. Would you be my date?" Elise was surprised at how natural it seemed to be asking.

Justin pretended to think for a second. "On one condition," he teased. "I won't really know anyone, but . . ." he said as they climbed into Elise's car. "I'll go if you let me pick you up in my T-bird."

Chapter
13

By nine o'clock Fiona's party was in full swing. Music was blasting from the stereo in the living room, and everyone was shouting to be heard above it. Emily was perched in a corner of the den by the sliding glass doors that led out onto the back deck, talking to Karen and her boyfriend, Brian Pierson. Actually, Karen was doing all the talking: Brian had his eyes closed and was nodding his head in time with the music, and Emily was absentmindedly toying with the buttons on her blue sweater. Ever since Scott had arrived at the party, she'd been nervous. She knew seeing him again would hurt, but she hadn't believed it would be so awkward.

So far, they had managed to keep a comfortable distance from each other. But Emily knew if she turned her head even a fraction of an inch, she'd be able to steal a glance at him from the corner of her eye. Part of her was tempted to look for him, but another part wanted to bolt out of the house and run the whole three miles home — race or no race.

She bent her knees and clasped her arms around them, trying to concentrate on what Karen was saying. But suddenly her eyes were drawn to the dining room, where she saw Scott loading up his plate with a second helping of pasta. Then he grabbed a can of soda and sat down by himself at the edge of the fireplace. Emily could tell he was nervous about the race tomorrow. His usual cheerful smile was missing, and he kept shifting his position uncomfortably on the plush carpet.

For one brief moment Emily considered going over and talking to him. After all, she might still be able to help him relax. Maybe they could work things out between them. She'd even settle for their becoming friends. Anything would be better than this hostile silence!

Emily sighed. Who was she kidding? The last time she'd tried to start a conversation with Scott, he'd stopped her with a cold, hard stare. What made her think he'd react differently tonight?

No, she thought as she ran her fingers through her hair in a futile gesture. It would be foolish to try to talk to him again. Scott wasn't himself anymore, and she'd only be leaving herself open for more anger and rejection. She definitely didn't want that.

Karen leaned over and lightly tapped her on the shoulder. Emily spun around, startled. "Earth to Emily!" Karen smiled. "Did you hear me tell you that Candy Hearts has gotten a dozen more letters since Tuesday?"

Emily's cheeks turned bright red, and she smiled politely at Karen. "Really. That's great!"

Brian realized she'd been distracted and laughed. "Nervous, huh?" He winked at her.

"Of course Emily's nervous," Karen said. "Wouldn't you be if you knew half the student body was depending on you to solve their romantic problems? Writing the Candy Hearts column is going to be a big responsibility," Karen stated flatly.

Brian poked her lightly in the ribs. "I don't doubt it. But *I* was talking about the half-marathon."

"Whoops . . . sorry." Karen clapped her hands over her mouth. "I keep forgetting there's life outside of the newspaper office."

"I know, I know," Brian groaned.

Emily leaned back against the sliding glass doors. She was glad they hadn't guessed the real reason she was acting like such an airhead. It wasn't nerves — or the race. It was all because of a tall, blond-haired boy with blue-gray eyes, who was sitting in the living room this very second, stuffing himself with pasta. She gave a little shudder. The glass on the door was chilly, and the cold penetrated her thin sweater. She felt like sneaking off somewhere to have a good, long cry. Maybe then she'd feel better. A party was not the right place to be tonight.

"Uh-oh. I think it's time to put on a new tape," Brian said, jumping up just as the music stopped. Fiona had asked Brian to play DJ for the evening.

"Excuse us, Emily." Karen flashed her an apologetic smile. "But Brian's new wave taste isn't really my idea of party music. I'd better go supervise the tape selection."

Emily nodded and turned to look out at the manicured lawn. The backyard appeared so quiet and peaceful. She got up off the plush carpet, and opening the doors just enough to squeeze through, stepped out onto the wooden deck.

It was a truly gorgeous night. The sky was clear, and each star glistened with a brilliant light of its own. Emily leaned against the deck railing and breathed in the crisp autumn air. Two figures were silhouetted beneath a large oak tree, their arms locked around one another. Seeing them reminded her of Laurie Bennington's party last spring, when she and Scott had wandered over to a pond in the backyard. The pond had a little waterfall, and opposite the waterfall was a hump-back bridge leading to a tiny island. Emily had crossed the bridge, and once on the island, she'd felt like she'd stepped into a fairyland, as if any minute, Prince Charming would come and carry her away. She told this to Scott, and he had immediately raced across the bridge and scooped her up in his arms.

Just thinking about that night brought tears to her eyes, and she bit her lip in an effort to force back the strong urge to cry. She had to stop thinking about Scott and how much she still loved him, or she would fall apart. And she didn't want that to happen — at least not until tomorrow. No matter how much it hurt, she had to hold herself together until after the race. Then she could let herself cry all she wanted. She'd have nothing else to do, now that she'd lost Scott. That was for sure.

The couple under the tree started walking toward the house, and as they neared the deck Emily could make out their voices. She recognized one immediately: It was Elise's. Her eyes narrowed, straining to see Elise. But who was the boy with her?

Suddenly they appeared out of the darkness and Emily gasped. It wasn't Ben who Elise was with. Of course it couldn't have been Ben — he was in New York. Suddenly all the hurt and anger she'd been feeling toward Scott was transferred to Elise. She couldn't believe Elise was seeing someone else — someone very attractive — while Ben was away! Were her boyfriend *and* her best friend both tossing love out the window? Emily's face grew tight, and her fingers curled around the deck railing.

Elise heard Emily's gasp and looked up. When she spotted her standing at the edge of the deck, she waved. 'Hi, Em. You enjoying the party?"

Emily put her hands on her hips and glared down at her friend. "Maybe I should ask you the same thing." Her eyes moved to Justin and back again.

The smile immediately faded from Elise's face. She dropped Justin's hand and whispered something in his ear. For a moment he looked confused, then he glanced up at Emily, nodded, and walked into the house. Elise waited until he had closed the door before slowly climbing the steps leading to the deck.

Emily stood straight as an arrow. "I saw that little scene by the maple tree," she said, trying to tame her anger. "What kind of game are you playing? When the cat's away, the mouse will play?"

Elise took a deep breath. "That's unfair, Emily," she said, walking over to a wooden bench. She bent over and brushed off a couple of dried leaves that had fallen on it before sitting down. "I know it looks like I'm cheating on Ben. But it's not what you think. Not really."

"No?" Emily whipped around to stare at her. "What is it then?"

"I've fallen in love with Justin."

Emily walked over to her. "Oh? When did this happen?"

A flush of color spread up Elise's neck and onto her face. "I don't know exactly. It's been growing slowly, and I didn't realize how serious it was until yesterday." She told Emily about their afternoon in Rosemont Park, and how after kissing Justin, she knew that this time it really was over with Ben. "Oh, Em, Justin makes me feel so wonderful. And he needs me. He really does."

"What about Ben? Doesn't he need you, too?"

Elise looked down and kicked the toe of her sneaker at an acorn lying by her foot. It rolled across the wooden planks and dropped over the edge of the deck. "Not the same way Justin does." A note of sadness crept into her voice. "Ben and I . . . well, science always comes first in his life. And I feel like a distant second."

Emily considered her friend's words. "Does Ben know you're no longer in love with him?"

"No . . . I . . . uh. . . . How could I tell him? He's in New York." Elise shook her head guiltily.

"He doesn't even know!" Emily sputtered, her

eyes widening. She leaned her hip against the deck railing. "Just when do you plan on telling him you've fallen in love with another guy?" she asked. There was a hard edge to her voice.

"As soon as he comes back, I guess."

"Well, for your sake, I hope Ben doesn't find out from someone else first. Your showing up at the party with Justin is bound to start people talking."

Elise's head snapped up. "Do you really think someone might call him?" She paled slightly. The last thing she wanted to do was hurt Ben. She still cared for him; she just wasn't in love with him anymore. Her eyes filled with tears.

"I don't know. Maybe." Emily stared down at her, stony-faced. "You should have thought of that possibility before inviting Justin."

"But why would anyone call Ben?" Elise asked, fear creeping into her voice. "I mean, what's wrong with my bringing a friend to the party?"

"Nothing's wrong!" Emily declared with an exasperated toss of her head. A wisp of hair fell onto her forehead and she tossed it back angrily. "Only Justin *isn't* just a friend — and people *aren't* stupid, Elise!" She took a quick, angry breath. "The least you could have done is waited until after you broke up with Ben before introducing your new boyfriend around!"

Elise felt her throat tighten. "All right, maybe I shouldn't have invited him. I'll give you that. But why are you so angry with me?" She stood up and looked at Emily. "I already told you I didn't plan on falling in love with Justin. It just happened. As my best friend, you should know I wouldn't intentionally hurt Ben." She stuffed her hands in her pockets.

"Look, all I know is that Ben trusted you, and you let him down."

Elise took a step back. The thought that Emily could be so angry with her was like a punch in the stomach. "I'm sorry if I disappointed you," she said after a moment, "but I'm only human."

"You are also very wrong." Emily glared at her. "Why don't you admit it? You know it's the truth."

"Stop it, Emily!" Elise said tightly. "I don't know what's bugging you, but I certainly don't intend to stand here any longer and listen to you play 'Dear Abby.' I've had it with your lecturing me on how I 'betrayed' my boyfriend. As far as I'm concerned you can save your moralizing for your newspaper column!" She took one last quick angry look at Emily and then spun around and walked into the house.

Emily stood there a moment, leaning against the porch wall. How could she have been so insensitive? Even if she'd been right, she never should have said the things she did to Elise. Tears started streaming down her cheeks, and she wiped the back of her hand across her face. Traces of mascara rubbed off on her skin. She'd just lost her best friend.

She hugged her arms around herself, trying to squelch the hollow feeling in her stomach. First Scott. Now Elise. She had alienated the two people she cared about most. It was also the second time that week that someone had told her to stop giving advice. Were they right? The more she thought about it, the more she wondered. Maybe she wasn't cut out to help people with their problems after all. Maybe she should go inside and tell Karen to find someone else to write the Candy Hearts column.

She sat down on the bench and buried her face in her hands. No. She couldn't go back into the house right now. She'd wait until Monday. Then she'd tell Karen.

Chapter
14

When Elise walked into the house, she saw Justin sitting on the living room floor with his back propped against the couch, talking to Jonathan, Karen, Marc, and Dee. She walked slowly over to the couch and sank down on the floor next to him.

Dee held out a plate to Elise filled with large pasta shells stuffed with cheese. "Want some?" she asked. "They're really terrific, believe me. If I could, I'd eat the whole plate!" she joked.

Elise looked at the shells and shook her head. "No, thanks." She wasn't very hungry, especially after her argument with Emily.

Karen took the plate from Dee and spilled a few shells onto the plate in front of her. "I don't mind if I do. Elise, we were just talking about Wendy Lewis," she said, handing the plate back. "Justin told us she was discharged from the hospital. Isn't that great news?" Her face broke out into a wide grin. "As soon as she comes back to school I'm going to ask her to write for *The Red and the Gold*. Think she'll be interested?"

Elise looked at Justin. "She might be," he said, balling up his napkin and tossing it into the fireplace where it was immediately engulfed in flames. "She liked the way you edited her article. She also liked your editorial in favor of installing a traffic signal." He clasped his hands behind his head and leaned back again. "In fact, she sent a copy of it along with her own letter to the mayor and the city council. Wendy wants them to do something about that intersection."

Jonathan leaned down from the couch, where he'd been sitting and waiting for Fiona to come back from the kitchen. "They should," he said forcefully. "So what did the mayor have to say?"

"So far, nothing," Justin shrugged. "Wendy hasn't gotten an answer from him or the city council."

"Maybe if we all wrote letters . . ." Marc mumbled through a mouthful of pasta.

"Better yet," Elise said, becoming caught up in the conversation. "Why don't we organize a protest march on the mayor's office? That'll make him sit up and take notice!"

Jonathan considered Elise's suggestion for a moment, then his smile widened into a grin. "Not a bad idea!" He leaned back on the couch and placed his elbow on the arm rest. "I can draw up a petition, and we'll ask all the students at Kennedy to sign it. Then we can let Wendy lead the march and present the petition to the mayor himself."

"Great!" Karen got to her knees, excited. "I'll cover the march for the school paper."

"And I'll take pictures!" Dee cried out.

Elise turned to Justin and saw him looking a little dazed. She figured he must be overwhelmed by how quickly they had planned the protest march. He'd never been involved in her friends' brainstorming sessions before, and didn't realize that they were always eager to support a good cause. They were some of the best organizers in all of Rose Hill!

"Justin, why don't you call Wendy and tell her what we're planning?" Karen said. He nodded in agreement and she started scribbling notes on her napkin. "I'll get Brian to announce the march over WKND." She paused and studied the list on her napkin. "Maybe I'll even call some of the local papers and see if they're interested in covering the march."

"While you're at it, call the *Washington Daily*," said Elise. "Wendy's father is the publisher. Maybe he'll send a reporter, too." Elise gave Justin a quick glance.

Karen nodded. "Good thinking. With all that publicity, the mayor will have to install a traffic signal."

Later that night, Justin sat behind the steering wheel, deep in thought. His eyes focused intently on the road, but his mind was still back at the party. He couldn't stop thinking about helping to organize the protest march: It would be the first positive step he'd taken since his brother's death.

114

It felt good not to be feeling sorry for himself any-more.

Elise reached over and touched his arm. "Justin, what are you thinking about?" she asked, once the silence had become unbearable.

He gave her a sidelong glance and reached down to capture her hand in his. It felt soft and warm and started her heart pounding. This was the first time since the party that he had touched her. It wasn't his fault: after her talk with Emily, Elise had been very careful not to get close to him in front of their friends. But she wasn't about to pull away now.

"I was thinking about tonight," Justin said softly. "I feel good about what we're planning." He put both hands back on the steering wheel. "I only wish I'd done something like this sooner. It's so obvious what needs to be done. I can't believe I've waited this long."

"Don't be so hard on yourself, Justin," Elise said lightly. "What's important is the fact that you're doing something now." She gave him an affectionate punch on the arm. Justin pretended to be hurt and began massaging his arm gingerly, a wounded look in his eyes. "I might also add that volunteering at the hospital wasn't exactly 'doing nothing.' Think of all the children you've helped. That's important, too."

He pulled the car up in front of Elise's house, and turned to face her. He could barely make out her face in the dark, so he flicked on the overhead light. Then he looked at her and shook his head. "Oh, Elise," he said, so tenderly that it gave her goosebumps. "You always make me feel good about myself. That's why it's wonderful to be with you."

Impulsively, Elise threw her arms around his neck, and her face was now only a few inches from Justin's. For a moment they just stared at each other. Then Elise felt herself leaning closer to Justin. Their mouths met, and his kiss, gentle at first, quickly grew stronger and more passionate.

Elise found herself wanting the kiss to go on forever, and when Justin pulled back to catch his breath, she sighed. "Oh, Justin," She stared into his beautiful blue eyes. "Am I dreaming this, or do you really care about me?"

He searched her face. "I . . . I care, Elise. I think I have ever since the day we met." He kissed her again, this time more gently. "After you listened to me talk about David, I knew I wanted to get to know you better." He squeezed her tightly to his chest. "In case you didn't realize, I love being with you."

Elise leaned her head against his forehead and sighed happily. She could hardly believe what she was hearing. Justin was saying everything she felt for him and she felt wonderfully light-headed. "Oh, Justin," she said, stroking the back of his neck. "And to think this is only the beginning."

Elise stepped out of the car and stood in the driveway, watching Justin drive off. It wasn't until his taillights had disappeared around the corner that she turned and headed for her house. The moment she did, she heard a strange sound, as if the heel of a shoe was scraping against the flagstone. She looked up and saw Ben standing on the front porch.

"Oh, no. . . ." She swallowed a small lump of terror in her throat. Ben had to have seen her kissing Justin. She wanted to melt into the sidewalk and die. She stood there, frozen in place, as he slowly stepped down from the porch and started walking toward her. She felt horrible. She had never intended for Ben to find out about Justin this way.

With a sinking sensation, she watched him close the gap between them. He stopped inches from her, close enough so she could see the sadness, hurt, and pain etched on his face. "Tell me I didn't see what I think I did, Elise," he pleaded. "Tell me my eyes are playing tricks on me."

Her heart stopped. "I can't," she answered guiltily. "Oh, Ben. I'm so sorry. I didn't know you were back from New York."

"I caught an early train," he said, raking his fingers through his hair. She noticed his hands were trembling. "I felt bad about missing Thanksgiving with you . . . and the party, too. . . . As soon as I got home, I called Fiona. She said you had already left, so I came here to wait. How long have you been seeing this guy?"

"Justin?"

"Is that his name?"

Elise nodded. "Justin McMaster. We met at the hospital. He works with the kids, too. And, well, his twin brother died a few months ago, and he's sort of having trouble accepting it."

"So, it's Florence Nightingale to the rescue?" Ben's voice was bitter.

"It's more than that," Elise said, wrapping her arms around her chest. She looked him straight in the eye. This wasn't how she had planned to say it, but now she had no choice. She had to tell Ben quickly and hope he understood that she never meant to hurt him.

She opened her mouth to begin, but before she had a chance to say anything, Ben reached for her hand. His eyes were clouded with pain. "What do you mean, 'more than that'?" he asked, pulling her into his arms. "You're not going to keep on seeing him? Are you?"

Elise's heart was in her throat. She swallowed and took a step back. Ben let his hands fall to his sides and stared into her eyes. "I've fallen in love with him," she said gently. Ben looked as if he'd just been slapped in the face. "I didn't mean to," she rushed on. "It just happened." Tears started to well up in her eyes, and just as she lifted her arm to wipe them away, Ben grabbed it violently.

"What about me, Elise? Don't you love *me* anymore?" His voice shook with emotion.

Before she could stop herself, tears began trickling down Elise's cheeks. "I'll always love you, Ben." Her voice trembled. "You're one of my favorite people in the world. But I'm not *in* love with you anymore."

He let his hand drop from hers and a puzzled look crossed his face. "Funny." He shook his head. "I never knew there was a difference."

"That's part of what's wrong between us," Elise said, her voice filled with sadness. "We care for each other, but we're not on the same wavelength. I don't think we ever really were, but we never bothered to notice. Not even last summer, when we came so close to breaking up."

"What?" Ben caught his breath. "What do you mean, we don't understand each other? You can't really mean that!" His face grew pale.

"Yes. Yes, I do." Elise wiped the tears from her cheeks. "Somehow, it didn't seem to matter before, but I've changed, Ben. I'm a different person from the one I was when we first started dating."

She glanced around the front yard and her eyes came to rest on the old oak tree. She remembered when she used to climb up into its branches in order to spy on Ben while he played with his Erector set. She couldn't have been more than seven or eight at the time, but they were good friends even then. She hoped they would still be friends after tonight.

She walked over to the tree and leaned her hip against its rough bark. Ben followed her over, then stood with his hands clinging to an overhead branch.

"Don't you see, Ben?" Elise folded her arms across her chest and hugged herself tightly. She felt so guilty and torn by her feelings for Ben and Justin. "You're a wonderful person. But the romance is gone. You and I just . . . we just don't belong together anymore." She looked pointedly at the ground while Ben's fingers tightened around the tree branch until his knuckles turned white.

"So, it's over between us."

Elise nodded. "I'm sorry, Ben. I really am.

It's. . . . I don't know what else to say." She started to cry again and turned toward the house.

Suddenly Ben's hands were on her shoulders and he forced her to turn around and face him. "Please, oh, please, Elise. I don't want to lose you."

She closed her eyes and dropped her head to her chest. It hurt to see Ben so upset — he wasn't acting like himself. With all her heart she wished she could look into his eyes, smile, and say it was all one big mistake. But it wasn't. It had been over between them for a long, long time. Someday Ben would realize that. "You're not really losing me," she sighed. "I'll always be your friend."

"My friend!" He snatched his hands back quickly, as if touching her made him sick. "That's not what I want!" he snapped, his eyes frigid as ice. Elise had never seen such hatred in his eyes before. And it cut deep into her soul.

"I'm sorry, Ben. Honest. I wish things could be different."

His shoulders tensed, Ben stood staring at her for a moment with his hands on his hips. "Yeah. I bet you do," he said, sneering. Then very quietly, he turned and walked away.

Chapter
15

The next morning Elise woke up early. A ray of golden sunlight was streaming in through her window, and she looked around her room, confused. If it was such a beautiful day, then why did she feel so sad? She sat up in bed and hugged her knees to her chest. Suddenly memories of last night came flooding back, and she let out a low moan and sank down onto her pillow. For a long while she lay staring up at the ceiling, a numb sadness filling her heart. She didn't feel like crying. She just felt hollow inside.

She got up out of bed and padded over to the window. Ben's two younger brothers were playing touch football in front of their house. Elise shook her head sadly. She still felt awful when she thought about how she had hurt Ben. But she knew she had done the right thing by breaking up with him. Just like she knew she had done the right thing when she went back to work at the hospital.

Elise stepped back from the window and did a few pirouettes around her room. As she did, she held her dark, wavy hair up off her neck. As bad as she felt about Ben, she couldn't wait to see Justin again. He was coming to pick her up around ten o'clock so they could watch the half-marathon. After last night, she certainly didn't have to worry about everyone seeing them together. Elise stopped in front of her dresser and let her hair fall to her shoulders. She picked up her hairbrush and, bending over, began brushing the soft curls with long, even strokes.

When the phone rang a few minutes later, it was Justin. She felt a rush of warmth when she heard his voice. "Hi," she said enthusiastically. "You ready for the race?"

"Well . . . I . . . actually, that's why I'm calling." He sounded a little distant. "There's a problem. Nothing serious," he added quickly. "It's just that I stopped by Wendy's house to tell her about the protest march, you know? And she wants me to stay and help her draft a petition."

"I thought Jonathan was going to do that," Elise said, trying not to sound disappointed. The strange tone of his voice bothered Elise. She'd never heard him sound so confused. She wondered if something was wrong with Wendy.

"Yes, well, so did I. But Wendy called him and — "

Elise forced herself to sound cheerful. "No problem. How long do you think it will take?"

"Well, I don't know," Justin hedged. "I'm not sure. A couple of hours maybe."

Elise heaved a sigh. She wanted to be understanding, but at the same time she really wanted to see Justin. "I guess that means you won't be taking me to the race."

Justin didn't say anything for a minute. When he finally did answer, his voice was so soft she had to strain to hear him. "No. I guess not. I'm . . . uh . . . sorry if I've messed up your plans."

It occurred to Elise that helping Wendy was probably something Justin needed to do. It was a way for him to erase some of his guilt about what had happened to David. She smiled. "It's okay. Don't worry about it. I'm sure I can find something to keep myself busy while you're working on the petition. Good luck — I hope it goes well!"

"Thanks, Elise." Justin sounded relieved. "I'll try and call you later."

Halfway across town Emily stood close to the starting line, trying to stretch out her tight muscles. It was already unusually warm for November, and the temperature was supposed to go even higher today. But that wasn't the reason she felt so worn out — it was because she hadn't slept well in days. Last night, in addition to seeing Scott's angry glare every time she closed her eyes, she saw Elise's face, too. It made her think about their fight, and what a terrible friend she had been. Instead of lecturing Elise, Emily knew she should have offered her support, as she had last summer when Elise thought she was beginning to feel something for Matt Jacobs.

She bent forward and let her hands dangle on

the ground. All around her runners were busy doing leg stretches and knee bends to limber up. She grasped her arms around her legs and pulled her head to her knees. She had already decided, after tossing and turning most of the night, that if Elise were at the finish line today, she would apologize to her. She'd even planned what she was going to say. Now that she had lost Scott, she wasn't about to let her best friend slip away, too.

"All runners please move to the starting line," a voice announced over the loudspeaker. Emily quickly straightened up into a standing position and looked around. This is it, she told herself, as a tense kind of excitement swirled in her stomach. She adjusted her pink headband and watched as hordes of runners, wearing everything from jogging suits to color-coordinated shorts and T-shirts, started scrambling for position. Emily let them weave around her. She didn't feel like getting caught up in the crush.

Emily spotted Scott a moment later, standing at the front of the line. His red Kennedy High T-shirt was already clinging to his back. But since there were a lot of runners separating them, she couldn't get a good look at his face.

The loudspeaker crackled again, and suddenly, without warning, Scott turned around and stared directly at her. Emily started to smile, then realized he wasn't looking at her, he was looking right through her. It was as if she weren't even there. Her whole body sagged, and she dropped her eyes to the ground.

When the gun went off, she felt herself being carried forward by a surge of people. As she fought to keep her balance, she noticed Scott, way out in front with the lead runners. Emily frowned. What was he trying to prove? Did he really think he could run with them for 13 miles? She kept her eye on him until he turned the first corner, then forced herself to block everything out and concentrate on her own race. The crowd around her had thinned out a little, and she settled into her own pace.

At the three-mile mark, she came to the first water station. Jeremy and Diana were among the volunteers handing out cups of water. Emily took one with a smile.

"At least one Kennedy student has sense," Jeremy quipped.

She took a gulp and tossed the cup to the side of the road. "What do you mean?" she called back.

"Scott ran past here a few minutes ago like a house on fire. He didn't even bother to stop for water!" Jeremy yelled, then ran after her with another cup of water. Once he caught up with Emily, he handed her the water, and she slowed down to sip thirstily.

Emily turned to Jeremy with a concerned look on her face. "Really?" she said. Emily was so winded she could hardly speak.

Diana joined up with them. "Doesn't Scott know how important it is to drink, especially on a warm day?" she asked. "Are you sure he didn't stop, Jeremy?"

"I'm positive," he answered. "I even tried chasing after him, but he was too fast for me."

Emily crumpled up her cup and tossed it into a

nearby trash can. "Thanks, anyway," she said, and pulled away from Jeremy. She immediately disappeared into the throng of other runners.

Checking her watch, she saw that she was still on pace. One by one, the miles began to disappear. She hoped Scott had had enough sense to slow down at one of the two water stations she had passed. If he waited until he was dying of thirst, it would be too late.

She started up a long, winding hill, the toughest part of the thirteen-mile course. Emily shortened her stride a little and, with her arms pumping, forced herself to concentrate on keeping her pace steady. A couple of times she felt herself falter, but each time she did, she would hear a voice call out encouragement from the sideline, and it gave her renewed energy. When she finally reached the top of the hill, she was elated. A few yards ahead was the eight-mile water station, and she could already see Dee waving her arms excitedly.

"You're right on time! Just like you planned," she exclaimed when Emily reached the table that was covered with little cups of water.

Emily shook her legs out a little and shrugged to loosen her muscles. "Amazing, isn't it?" she said, breathing hard. "How far ahead is Scott? How does he look?"

Marc walked over and handed her another cup of water. She took it and poured the water over her head. Marc laughed and checked his watch. "I'd say he staggered by about ten or fifteen minutes ago. And he definitely did not look good," he added. "His face was a little on the pale side and his eyes were sort of glazed over."

Emily's eyes widened. "Did he stop for water?" Marc shook his head.

"That's crazy! He's going to hurt himself!" She gasped. "We've got to do something!"

"I know. But what?" Marc asked in a worried voice.

Emily grabbed his arm. "Try and catch up with him, Marc. Please," she begged. "Get him to drink some water. Pour it into him if you have to. It's the only way he'll make it to the finish line."

Marc stared at her for a second, then broke into a run. Scott was lucky he had friends who still cared about him, thought Emily. He was behaving like a total fool!

She turned to Dee. "Tell Marc I said thanks!"

"I will. You go ahead," Dee said. "You're still in this race!"

"Okay, see you later," she said with as much enthusiasm as she could muster and continued the race.

When she finally neared the finish line and saw her friends gathered along the road, her face broke into an ear-to-ear grin. Fiona was holding a large cardboard sign that said: GO, EMILY! The rest of the crowd was making a real event of cheering her on.

She crossed the finish line, and the cheers turned into a roar. She quickly checked her watch and saw she had finished the race in one hour and fifty-three minutes. Even though she hadn't set a world record, her time was nothing to be ashamed of.

Jonathan ran up and grabbed her in his arms.

She was all hot and sweaty, but he didn't seem to care. He swung her around and around, yelling, "You did it! You did it!"

Soon everyone was hugging and congratulating her, and Emily felt wonderful. She had finished her first race. After walking around for a bit, stretching and cooling down, she pulled off her pink headband and started to shake out her hair. She drank some juice and more water. It occurred to her that she hadn't seen Scott anywhere. She tore herself away from her friends and started scanning the crowd. Fiona sensed instantly who she was looking for and walked over to her.

"Where's Scott?" Emily asked, her eyes filled with concern.

Fiona shook her head. "He had to drop out of the race, Em. He was dehydrated and exhausted. Marc and Dee drove him home."

Emily's face paled. "Will he be all right?" she asked, her blue eyes now dark with worry. If anything happened to Scott. . . . She closed her eyes and willed herself not to cry.

Fiona sensed her anguish and spoke up quickly. "I think he's okay, except for his pride," she reassured Emily.

Taking a deep breath, Emily pushed a wisp of hair off her cheek and nodded. She was sure Scott was mortified about not being able to finish the race, but at least he wasn't seriously hurt. The tense knot at the back of her neck loosened a little, and saying good-bye to Fiona, she slowly walked over to her car.

As she drove out of the parking lot, it occurred to her that she hadn't seen Elise at the finish line.

Chapter
16

Emily murmured an apology as she brushed past a group of students and hurried down the hallway. She wanted to find Elise before the first period bell rang. She hadn't gotten around to calling her over the weekend. After the race, she had fallen asleep and hadn't woken up until late. Then she'd had to spend the rest of the weekend doing homework.

Her footsteps slowed as she neared her friend's locker. Elise was standing in front of it, her forehead resting on the cool gray metal, as she dialed the combination on her lock. Emily brushed her hands nervously against her jeans and took another step forward. Just then, a group of seniors approaching from the other direction spotted her and rushed over to shake her hand and clap her on the back. "Hey, congratulations!" "Great job!" "You gave Kennedy a good name!"

Emily felt more than a little embarrassed. She

wasn't used to this kind of attention. She was also somewhat distracted, and when the seniors finally moved on, she quickly glanced over toward Elise's locker. Elise happened to be looking up, and their eyes met. They stood there, silently staring at each other until Elise spun around and angrily stormed off in the opposite direction.

It was no use. Elise was never going to forgive her. She glanced at the wall clock, trying not to cry. There were only five minutes left until first period. Should she talk to Karen now or wait until lunchtime or after school? She debated with herself a moment, then turned and headed for *The Red and the Gold* office. It was going to make her late for history class, but she had to get it over with before she lost her courage.

Emily walked into the newspaper office and straight over to Karen's desk. Karen was leaning over the layout of this week's edition of *The Red and the Gold*, trying to figure out how to squeeze a three-page story onto two pages. As soon as she saw Emily, Karen looked up. "Hi, Em. What are you doing here so early?"

For a moment, Emily just stood there, not sure how to begin. Karen sat back in her chair and regarded her steadily. "I . . . I have to talk to you," she finally said. "I'm not going to be able to write the Candy Hearts column. I'm sorry, but I just can't do it." She jammed her hands into the roomy pockets of her green safari pants.

Karen folded her arms across her chest and exhaled slowly. "How come? Something must have happened to make you change your mind."

Emily hesitated, then shook her head. "Not really." She saw Karen's eyebrows go up and knew she didn't believe her. But for some reason she still couldn't bring herself to tell Karen the truth. It hurt too much. She dropped her eyes. "It's . . . it's just causing too many problems."

Karen pushed her glasses onto the top of her head and stood up. Then she walked slowly over to the window. "Okay," she said, staring out at the quad. "If that's the way you feel, I can't force you to write it. But you can't quit on me just like that!" She spun around and snapped her fingers. "You've got to at least give me time to find a replacement."

Emily fiddled with the large clip in her hair. "How long will you need?"

Karen went back to her desk and picked up a pencil. She began tapping it against her hand. "I'm not sure. How about two weeks? Does that sound fair? I need to have the first and second installments ready right away."

Emily gave a little shrug. "Sure, I'll finish out the next two issues." She couldn't really argue with that.

"Good." Karen perched on the edge of her desk, and slipped the pencil behind one ear. She looked down at the layout spread across her desk. The Candy Hearts column was being given half a page. "Will it be a problem for you to come back during lunch today?" she asked, after a moment. "I think we should talk about how many letters you're planning to answer for the next two columns."

"I'll be here," Emily said, just as the tardy bell rang. "And thanks for being so understanding," she called, racing out the door. If she hurried, she might still be able to slip into class without anybody noticing.

On her way back to *The Red and the Gold* office later, Emily stopped by the cafeteria. She needed to pick up a sandwich and something to drink, and she was also hoping she might see Scott. At least she knew he was in school today. Dee had told her that after she managed to sneak into history class a few seconds late. But she wanted to see for herself that he was okay. She edged past a table of noisy sophomores, to the place where her crowd usually sat. It was nearly full, but Scott wasn't there. Elise wasn't there, either.

Fiona smiled and waved at Emily from across the table. Emily smiled back. "Hi, you guys. Where's everyone else?" she asked, meaning Scott, but not wanting to come right out and ask for him. Fiona apparently thought she was asking about Elise, because she pointed to the end of the table where Ben was sitting slumped down in his chair, and pressed her fingers to her lips for Emily to be quiet. Ben's face was hidden behind a book, but his posture displayed the mood he was in. Fiona was trying to tell her that Elise was probably off somewhere with Justin. Word had already gotten around about her and Ben breaking up.

"Grab a seat," Jonathan said, then realized there were no empty chairs. "Wait, you can have mine. I've got to return a book to the library. I might as well do it now." He started to get up, but Emily stopped him.

"That's okay," she said. "I can't stay. I have a meeting with Karen in a few minutes."

"Does that mean what I think it does?" Jeremy asked, munching on a potato chip. "If so, it's about time. A lot of people are waiting for Candy Hearts to help them solve their romantic problems."

Jonathan chuckled. "Yeah, Karen told me that once word got out you were writing the column, dozens of letters came pouring into her office. You have quite a reputation around Kennedy, you know."

Emily could feel herself blushing. "Well, I hate to disappoint everyone, but I'm only going to be writing Candy Hearts for two issues."

"Two issues!" Jonathan exchanged surprised glances with everyone at the table. "What do you mean? I thought Candy Hearts was going to be a regular weekly column!"

"Oh, it is," Emily reassured him. "It's just that I won't be writing it."

"Why not?" everyone yelled at once.

Emily had expected a reaction, but the sudden shout startled her. She jumped and her notebook slipped out of her arms. She bent to pick it up. "I . . . uh . . . I told Karen I didn't want to do it," she said, straightening some pages that had fallen out.

"You what!" Fiona demanded. She scrambled to her feet and came around the table. She planted her hands on her hips and looked Emily square in the face. "Will you please explain?"

Emily gulped. "I just don't think I'm cut out to give advice, that's all." She held her notebook against her chest and dropped her head. Her long dark hair fell down over her face like a shield. "Lately, every time I've tried to help someone, it's come out all wrong. Look at what happened when I tried to help Scott," she added, unable to keep the hurt out of her voice.

Fiona turned to Jonathan as if to say "Say something, please." He looked back and shrugged.

"Anyway," Emily continued, "I've decided to quit while I'm ahead — and before I lose *all* of my friends. As soon as Karen finds a replacement for me, I'll be out of the advice business." She started backing away. "Now if you'll all excuse me." She turned and walked over to the cafeteria line.

The line was long, but Emily needed to get something to eat, otherwise she'd never make it through the day. She picked up a tray and let her eyes scan the cafeteria. It was jammed, and the din of voices trying to make themselves heard over the noontime radio show was deafening. She was still hoping to spot Scott. After a moment, it occurred to her that he might be eating his lunch in the quad. It had to be a lot quieter out there. But then she realized it was much too cold outside: Overnight the temperature had dropped dramatically. Besides, now that Thanksgiving had come and gone, everyone was thinking winter. Nobody would think of eating outside —

but then again, Scott had been doing some pretty crazy things lately.

A sudden break in the music made everyone stop talking and look up. Brian's voice came out loud and clear over the loudspeakers. "Attention, students! This is Brian Pierson, taking a break from my excellent taste in music to bring you an important announcement. As you all undoubtedly know by now, there is going to be a protest march to the mayor's office this afternoon. The reason for the march is to convince the mayor to install a much-needed traffic signal at the corner of Rose Hill Avenue and Everett Street. If you haven't already done so — and even if you can't march with us to the mayor's office — please sign the petition hanging in the main lobby before three o'clock today. We need all the signatures we can get. And yours *will* make a difference."

People started to get up and talk again in the cafeteria. "Wait! I'm not finished yet," Brian said, as if he had heard them. "I'd like to take another minute of your time to offer congratulations to two Kennedy students, both of whom accomplished something special this weekend. First, congratulations to Ben Forrest for winning honorable mention at the New York Science Fair. And the same to Emily Stevens, for setting a record for girls her age in the Rose Hill half-marathon. Kennedy is proud of both of you!"

As soon as Jonathan walked into the library, he spotted Scott sitting off in a corner all by himself. He was slumped down in his chair, nibbling on a sandwich. Everything about him gave the impression that he wanted to be left alone.

Jonathan remembered feeling the same way last spring after his fight with Fiona. But Emily had ignored the wall he'd built around himself and helped him understand that everyone makes mistakes now and again. He dropped off his book at the return desk and headed across the large, airy room. Maybe what Scott needed was someone to talk to, to help him see that what he'd done was foolish, but also that dropping out of the race wasn't the end of the world.

He pulled up a chair and sat down at the table next to Scott. "Hey, pal. How come you're eating your lunch in the library?" Jonathan asked.

Scott looked up and sighed. "I'm trying to hide, okay?"

"Why?"

"Wouldn't you, if you had just humiliated yourself in front of all your friends?"

Jonathan raised an eyebrow. "C'mon, Scott, lighten up already. So what if you blew the race? It's over. Forget it!"

"I wish I could. But after hearing Brian's announcement as I walked into the lunchroom, I decided to take off. I couldn't stand to face everyone after hearing that."

"Do you really mean everyone, or just Emily?"

Scott shrugged. "Her especially. She was right all along, you know. I really did overdo it." He leaned his elbows on the long oak table and put his head between his hands. "I don't know what came over me. But after the way I've been acting

— not to mention some of the things I said to her — she probably hates my guts. Not that I blame her. I've been such a jerk."

"I'll go along with that," Jonathan joked, in an effort to make Scott laugh. But it didn't work: Scott only nodded in agreement.

"If only I had taken Emily's advice. I wouldn't be sitting here right now feeling like the biggest loser in the world."

"You might try telling *her* that," Jonathan suggested.

Scott's head snapped up, and he shook his head vehemently. "Who are you kidding? She'd only laugh in my face."

"I don't think so." Jonathan leaned forward. "In fact I think it would make her feel a whole lot better."

"How?"

"Well, I just saw her in the cafeteria. She told me she was quitting the paper," he said. "And I think it might be because of something you said to her."

"Me!" Scott raised his eyebrows.

Jonathan nodded.

Scott thought for a minute. Jonathan made sense. "Oh, boy! I really blew it, didn't I?" He rested his head in his hands. "Not only did I drive away the only girl I've ever really loved, but I managed to destroy her confidence in the process."

Jonathan nodded again. "She thinks because she failed with you, she'll fail with everyone."

"But she didn't fail! She was right!" Scott raised his voice and the librarian looked up. She put a finger to her lips in warning. He dropped his voice to a whisper and continued. "I've got to talk to her!"

Jonathan laid a restraining hand on his arm. "Would it help if I told you she's meeting with Karen Davis in a few minutes?" He smiled.

Scott looked at him for a moment, then started gathering his stuff. "Thanks, pal," he said. "I owe you one."

Chapter
17

Karen handed Emily the Candy Hearts box filled with letters and directed her to an empty desk by the window. "Why don't you finish going through these, and then pick out five or six you want to respond to in your first column. Then we can type up the letters to get an idea of how much space you'll have left over for your answers." Karen started back to her own desk, then stopped as if she had just remembered. "Oh . . . you might also check the submission box outside. Just in case." She smiled secretively. "I think I saw someone drop a letter in a few minutes ago. Who knows, it might be urgent."

Emily put her sandwich down on the desk and walked out into the hallway. Hanging on the wall just outside *The Red and the Gold* office was the Candy Hearts submission box. She unlocked the hinged lid and reached inside the box. Almost immediately her hand came to rest on what felt like a thin envelope. She pulled it out, and turned it over to see the name *Candy Hearts* scribbled on the front of the envelope.

Her brow furrowed, and for a few seconds she just stood there, staring down at the bold handwriting. Was it possible? She went back inside to her desk, settled down in her chair, and ripped open the envelope. Inside was a single sheet of paper.

> *Dear Candy Hearts,*
>
> *I need your advice. Recently, my girl friend tried to stop me from doing something really stupid. Only instead of listening to her, I got angry and said some pretty terrible things. I want to apologize for being such a jerk, and tell her that I love her. Will you help me?*
>
> *Scott*
>
> *P.S. I don't think I can wait until the paper comes out for your answer. Please meet me in the library. Hurry!*

Emily clutched the letter against her chest. She didn't know whether to laugh or cry. *He loves me!* She felt a rush of adrenaline and before she realized what she was doing, Emily found herself grabbing up her things and heading for the library.

"Does this mean I can stop looking for another columnist?" Karen said. She looked up as Emily passed by her desk. There was a big smile on her face.

Emily stopped and looked at Karen. "I certainly hope so!" She grinned and ran over to give Karen a quick, friendly hug. "I'll be back during study period, and I'll let you know then. Is that okay?"

"Far be it from *me* to stand in the way of true love," Karen said, winking at Emily.

When Emily found Scott, he was almost hidden among the stacks of books in the reference section. He was leaning back against a set of shelves, with his arms across his chest, staring straight ahead at nothing in particular. She was so glad to see him that it took her a moment to notice how drawn and tired he looked. The color was gone from his cheeks, and his eyes were all puffy, as if he hadn't slept in days.

She swung her hair back over her shoulder and walked slowly down the narrow aisle. Emily was glad she had worn her hair down today — that was the way Scott liked it best.

"Hi," she said quietly when Scott turned and saw her coming toward him.

Scott leaned his head back against the books and closed his eyes for an instant. "You came." He let out a deep sigh that let Emily know he'd been afraid she wouldn't show up.

She wanted to reach out to him, to let him know she would always be around if he needed her, but she stifled the urge. There were things they had to settle between them first.

Scott looked at her fondly, and still leaning against the bookcase, reached for her hand. "You're really here." He gently squeezed her fingers.

Emily bit her lip. "Well, your letter did say you couldn't wait."

"No . . . I couldn't." He gave her a sweet smile that almost broke her heart. "I owe you a huge apology," he went on, his voice thick with emotion. "I'm really sorry I blew up at you that day at the track. I didn't mean any of the things I said. Really."

"Good. I'm glad."

"You really mean that?" A gleam of hope shone in his blue-gray eyes.

Emily nodded. If Scott only knew that she'd been dying to hear him say those very words!

"I should have listened to you." He turned her hand over and stared at her palm as if he was trying to read her fortune. "That's pretty obvious now. But I was so scared! I was sure I wasn't going to do well in the race. And . . . well, now I feel like such a failure."

"Don't, Scott," Emily responded quickly. She pulled her hand free and rested her hands on his shoulders. "Everybody makes mistakes. It's part of how we learn. Just watch — in a few days everyone will have forgotten all about the race."

Scott raised his head and his blue-gray eyes focused on her intently, as if he were looking into her soul. "What about you? Will you be able to forgive and forget everything that happened between us this past week?"

"I already have," she said softly, reaching to push a few strands of blond hair off his forehead. Scott took her hand and gently kissed it before encircling her waist with his arms. "I love you, Emily. I never stopped."

Emily closed her eyes and let her head fall against his shoulder. It felt so good to be back in Scott's arms. "I love you, too," she whispered. And to prove exactly how much, she tilted her face up and kissed him on the lips.

Scott responded passionately, and what started out as a sweet, gentle kiss, grew more intense. Emily wrapped her arms more tightly around Scott's neck. It was amazing, but in the space of one short moment, all the distance that had been between them this past week had vanished.

"Emily," Scott sighed, pulling away. He took her face between his hands and made her look him in the eye. "There's something else we need to talk about."

A puzzled look crossed her face. "What?"

"Candy Hearts."

Her blue eyes widened. "What about it?"

"I want you to promise me you won't quit the column," he said seriously. "I really believe you give good advice. And while I don't enjoy being in the limelight myself, I am sort of looking forward to basking in *your* glory."

Emily laughed softly. "Really?" She was so light and giddy she felt almost dizzy. "Tell you what," she said, giving Scott her most beautiful smile. "I'll promise if you kiss me one more time."

Chapter
18

Elise looked up and saw Justin standing near the auditorium. He looked so handsome in his baggy white cotton sweater and baggy army fatigue pants. Her footsteps quickened. She was so happy to see him again. She'd been upset when he hadn't called her back last weekend, but when she found his note in her locker this morning, she didn't really care anymore.

"Hi!" she said excitedly as she came up next to him.

He looked directly at her and nodded hello, but he didn't reach out to hug her or take her hand. Elise took a deep breath. It was obvious something was wrong.

"Let's go inside where we can talk." Justin gestured toward the heavy wooden doors leading into the auditorium. He stuffed his hands into his pants' pockets and started walking. Elise hesitated a minute, then followed him inside and over to the last aisle.

The auditorium was empty and dark, except for a single overhead light shining down on the center of the stage. Justin slipped into a seat in the back row, and without looking at her, slid down in his chair and folded his arms across his chest.

"Elise, I think we have a problem." He sighed heavily.

She leaned back against the row of seats in front of him and stared at Justin in disbelief. "We do?" Elise had no idea what he was talking about.

He let his head fall back against the seat and met her gaze. "Actually, *I* have the problem, but it concerns you."

Elise's eyes widened. "Justin, what are you talking about?"

He took a deep breath, and unfolding his arms, leaned forward with his elbows on his knees. "I'm not sure how to tell you this," he said, staring down at his hands. "But the other night I wasn't totally honest with you. I — I mean I let you say things, and I'm not sure I should have."

Elise felt all the color drain from her face. "I don't understand. What things?" She began to tremble.

"Things about us. How I feel." Justin cleared his throat. "Don't you see, Elise? For the past six months I've let life go on around me. It was dumb. I realize that now . . . thanks to you." He sat up straight and looked at her. "But that's all behind me now. In fact I took the first big step over the weekend and resigned from the hospital — "

Elise gasped. "Is that what this is all about?" She sat down in the seat next to Justin. "You're afraid I'll be upset because you want to leave the hospital? That's crazy! We'll still be able to see each other."

Justin shook his head quickly. "Wait, Elise. You don't understand."

Slowly the smile faded from her face. "I don't?"

"No. That's only *part* of what I want to tell you."

Elise blinked. She was afraid to hear the rest.

"It's all my fault." Justin sagged back against his seat. "I like you, Elise, and when I said you were one of the most wonderful people in the world, I meant it. I also meant it when I kissed you. But love. . . ." He shifted uncomfortably. "I'm not sure I'm ready to commit myself to one girl yet. That's why I never called you back this weekend."

Elise drew in her breath sharply and closed her eyes. She suddenly felt as if the ground was slipping out from under her. This couldn't be happening. Justin wasn't really telling her this. She sat gripping the seat in front of her as if it would keep her from falling.

"Elise?" Justin leaned toward her. "Please look at me."

She opened her eyes. They were filled with tears. "What exactly are you trying to tell me, Justin?" she asked. "Have you been seeing someone else?"

He glanced down at the floor. "No. Not really. But after Wendy and I finished drafting the petition, I took her to the China Bowl. We had a deal, remember?" He smiled weakly. "Anyway, it was a great afternoon. We had a lot of laughs together. To make a long story short, I asked her out for a date Friday night."

Elise froze. That was the last thing she expected to hear. Or was it? She remembered back to the afternoon she and Justin had watched Wendy in physical therapy. She would have suspected something then, if she hadn't been so blind.

"I'm sorry if I've hurt you, Elise. I didn't do it intentionally. You've got to believe me. But, you know, I've always had a secret crush on Wendy. I just never did anything about it." He swallowed hard. "I mean, I remember how much I liked her when David took her out. They only dated a couple of times, and now David is gone. . . ." He paused.

Elise tried to speak, but there was a huge lump in the back of her throat. She folded her arms across her chest and hugged herself tightly.

Justin placed a warm hand on her forearm. "It isn't that I don't care for you, Elise. I do. Your friendship means a lot to me, and I'd feel awful if I lost it. Please don't hate me." He leaned over and kissed her gently on the cheek.

Chapter
19

As soon as the final bell rang, everyone started gathering in the quad for the march to the mayor's office. The weather was perfect — crisp and sunny, with just a trace of wind.

Emily glanced up at Scott as they hurried toward the main entrance. She didn't have to look at her watch to know that they were late. Scott had cornered her in a nook behind the west staircase when she came out of last period English for a quick kiss. Only one kiss had led to another, and another. They would probably still be there if the school janitor hadn't spotted them on his way up to the third floor.

"Are you sure you want to go on this march?" Scott asked Emily as they neared the trophy case in the front hallway.

Emily tightened her fingers around his waist. "Don't you?"

"The truth?" Scott stopped and backed her

against the wall. Emily didn't put up any resistance. "I'd rather be alone with you."

"Me, too," she said dreamily. "But everyone's expecting us."

"Yeah, I know." Scott let out a long, languid sigh and dropped his hands from around her shoulders. "Later." He looked furtively around to see if anyone was watching, before bending down to quickly kiss her on the lips.

Emily tugged at his shirt. "C'mon, Scott. You aren't playing fair."

Once outside, they found Karen and Fiona standing on the steps, handing out cardboard picket signs to anyone who wanted to carry one. A small cluster of students was gathered around, laughing and clapping each other playfully on the back. Emily looked at Scott, her eyes shining. He gave her a bright smile and together they made their way over to Fiona.

"Just in the nick of time!" Fiona shouted above the noise from the crowd. "Any minute now, I'm going to run out of signs!"

"I can see why," Scott said. "It looks like the whole student body has turned out for the march!"

Emily took the sign Fiona handed her and scanned the quad. Scott was right: Everyone seemed to be here. She looped the string attached to the sign around her neck and followed him down the steps into the milling crowd. For a second Emily thought she heard someone call to her, so she lifted her hand to shield her eyes from the sun and stood on her tiptoes looking around. She could just see Jeremy standing by the wall surrounding the flagpole, beckoning to her. She nudged Scott and they started over toward him.

Diana and Marc were with Jeremy. Diana had her arm linked through Jeremy's and from the expression on her face, Emily could tell she was very excited about the march. Marc, meanwhile, was carefully supporting Dee, who stood on top of the retaining wall, busily snapping pictures of the crowd. Emily held up her sign when Dee aimed the camera in her direction, and saw an amused smile play across her friend's mouth. Dee adjusted her telephoto lens and snapped a quick succession of pictures.

"Did we miss anything?" Emily asked, once they reached the flagpole.

"Not really." Diana shook her head and her long blonde hair swung around to brush her cheeks. "Jonathan went to get his car. And we're still waiting for Wendy Lewis."

"Leave it to Jonathan to graciously offer the use of his car," Scott joked. "Not only does he have the privilege of escorting Wendy, the star of the show, to the mayor's office — but he gets to *ride* there, instead of walking his feet off with the rest of us!"

They all laughed, except Dee who had crouched down on the wall and was quickly loading another roll of film into her camera. She looked every bit the news photographer with her camera case slung over one shoulder and her pockets bulging with extra rolls of film. Emily turned to say something to Dee, when out of the corner of her eye she noticed Ben, standing by himself, with his head down and his hands shoved deep into his jacket pockets. He looked very distant, as if he was purposely trying to avoid meeting anyone's eyes, and Emily suspected it must be because he was still hurting from what had happened with Elise. She was debating whether or not to go over and talk to him, when Ben suddenly started to walk away. Emily looked around, expecting to see Elise somewhere close by, but she wasn't. Why did Ben take off so quickly?

Emily craned her neck and started searching the quad for Elise. She was still hoping they could hug and make up or at least just apologize to each other. Emily felt a twinge of dismay as she surveyed the groups of kids huddled together on the grass. It wasn't like Elise to miss the march, especially when it was as important as this was. She was always a champion of good causes. Maybe she was too embarrassed to face Ben? No, Emily doubted that. Elise might feel badly about hurting Ben, but that wasn't enough to keep her from marching. There had to be another reason she hadn't shown up.

As if she was reading her mind, Dee bent over to whisper into Emily's ear, "Look over there." She pointed in the direction of the main entrance.

Emily turned around to see what Dee was talking about and blinked her eyes in disbelief. Standing in front of the school, very close to each other, were Justin McMaster and Wendy Lewis. They smiled for the cameras from the local TV station, then quickly turned back to each other. Emily couldn't help but notice that in the midst of all the chaos, and with everyone looking at them, Wendy and Justin seemed aware only of each other.

The TV crew started filming as Wendy very carefully made her way down the steps. She had on a yellow jacket and a blue denim miniskirt that failed to hide the brace on her leg. Emily couldn't help but admire her courage. It took guts to put yourself on display and stick up for what you really believed was right.

"Am I seeing things, or is that Justin McMaster with Wendy?" Diana turned to Emily, her eyebrows arched. They all knew Justin from the party.

Emily nodded. "It's Justin."

"I don't understand," Diana whispered. "I thought he was seeing Elise. What happened?"

Emily shrugged. She had no idea, but judging by the way he was looking at Wendy, it was just as well Elise wasn't around.

"Hey, are you all right?" Scott asked, putting his arm around her shoulder.

Emily flushed. For a moment she didn't know what to say. "Scott." She tilted her face up to his and swallowed hard. "I can't go on the march with you. I've got to find Elise."

"Right now?"

Emily nodded. "It's urgent."

"I don't get it." He shook his head. "I thought you two were on the outs."

"We are." Emily shifted uncomfortably. "But I still care about her, and I think she may need a friend right now."

Scott looked down at Emily and considered her remark. "Okay, suppose she does?" he said

152

gently. "How can you be sure she'll want to talk to *you*?"

"I can't," Emily murmured. "That's another reason I've got to find her. She and I have never had a fight like this before, and I hate the way it's making me feel."

Her voice caught in her throat, and she began to twist her fingers nervously. Scott reached for her hand and wrapped his fingers around hers. "I know how you feel, but can't it wait until after the march?"

Emily felt her heart tug. What if Scott didn't understand? The last thing she wanted to do was threaten their relationship again. She searched his eyes, hoping they would tell her what he was thinking. But she couldn't read their expression. She closed her eyes for an instant, aware that the students' chanting was quickly becoming muffled. They must be starting to turn onto Rose Hill Avenue. She had to make her decision quickly.

She took a deep breath and very slowly began to remove the picket sign from around her neck. "I've got to go *now*, Scott. Please understand." She handed him the sign.

For the longest moment he just stared at her. Emily felt for sure she had blown it. She was about to change her mind — to tell him she would go on the march — when he reached out and took the sign very gently from her hands.

"Go ahead, Em. It's okay." He gave her a lopsided smile. "I was sort of hoping we could spend the afternoon together, but I understand. Besides, one of the things I've always loved about you is that you care about people." He held out his arms to her.

He did understand! Emily felt a warm rush of happiness fill her every pore. "Oh, Scott, I love you," she said as he drew her to him.

"Enough to meet me at Sticky Fingers later? Everyone's heading over there after the march."

She pulled back and took his face between her hands. "I'll be there, I promise." She leaned forward and kissed him softly on the lips. And at that moment she loved Scott more than she ever had before.

Chapter
20

Emily pedaled her bicycle furiously down Everett Street, and when she came to Elise's house, she turned into the driveway and braked to a stop. Across the street a group of young boys were playing a game of touch football. As she leaned her bike up against the house, she saw one of them throw a long, high pass across the front lawn. Another player scrambled to catch it, but before he could, a third boy lunged into the air and came away with the ball.

Emily shook her head in amusement and started up the flagstone path. But as soon as she reached the door, the smile faded from her face. What was she going to say to Elise? She hung back a moment and closed her eyes. She had to make her friend understand that she was really sorry for turning on her the way that she had. She took a couple of deep breaths and rang the doorbell. When no one answered, she rang again.

Elise had to be home: her mother's car was in the driveway.

Just then the front door swung open and Emily found herself face to face with Elise.

"Em!" Elise exclaimed, and fell into her arms.

Emily hesitated a second, then hugged her tightly. "Oh, Elise. I'm so sorry. I was a terrible friend the night of the party. I never should have said the things I did. I just — "

"Got a little crazy for a minute?"

Emily pulled back a little, her blue eyes wide. "Yes. That's exactly what happened. Will you forgive me?"

Elise gave her a shy smile. "I'm talking to you, aren't I?" She motioned for Emily to step inside, then pushed the front door closed and walked over to the staircase.

Emily breathed a long sigh of relief. "Thanks, Elise. I really hated it when you were mad at me."

"Me, too." Elise sank down onto the bottom step. She put her arms around her knees and leaned her head against the railing. "It was awful. I didn't know . . . I mean, there was no one I could *talk* to." Her shoulders began to shake, and by the time Emily sat down, tears were already rolling down her cheeks.

Emily wrapped her arm around Elise. "Is it Justin?" she asked quietly.

A shadow flitted across her friend's face. "H-how did you know?"

"I saw him with Wendy Lewis before the march. And — uh — it was sort of obvious that they care about each other."

Elise regarded her for a moment. "I know." She sagged back against the steps. "Justin told me. Oh, Em." She hid her face in her arms. "I'm so embarrassed. I made such a fool out of myself!"

Emily nodded sympathetically. "There seems to be a lot of that going around lately," she said, thinking of herself and Scott.

"But how could I have been so stupid?" Elise wailed painfully.

Emily glanced down at her hands. "I don't understand. I mean — well — it may be none of my business, but what did you do that was so terrible?"

"I let myself fall in love with Justin." Elise's voice dropped to a whisper. "It's crazy. But I was so sure he loved me back. Just — just the way he kissed me. It was so — different. And he kept telling me I was the most wonderful person in the world." Her lips began to tremble. "Oh, Em," she cried, and buried her face in her arms. Tears of anguish flowed from her eyes.

Emily got up and walked into the guest bathroom and returned a moment later with a box of tissues. "I don't get it." She yanked a couple out and stuffed them into Elise's hand. "Are you telling me Justin *lied* to you?"

Elise blew her nose. "No." She shook her head slowly from side to side. "He didn't lie. I did — to myself."

Emily sat back down on the steps. "Did you also lie to yourself about Ben?" she asked quietly.

Elise glanced up and met Emily's eyes. "No.

In fact that's one of the few things I *was* honest with myself about. I know I hurt Ben, but breaking up with him was the right thing to do."

"You're sure about that? No regrets?"

"No regrets," Elise sniffled. "I just hope that someday he and I can be friends again."

"What about Justin?" Emily asked.

A shadow of sadness fell across Elise's face. These past few weeks had been a learning experience for her. She'd come to understand a lot about herself. Like how fulfilling it was to do something good for other people — and that while being in love was wonderful, losing a boyfriend wasn't the end of the world.

"Right now, I hurt a lot," she admitted. "But I don't regret having fallen in love with Justin. If it hadn't been for him, I might never have realized that things between Ben and me had been wrong since last summer." She folded her arms across her chest and hugged herself tightly. Another tear slid down her cheek. "It's really my own fault — I wanted to feel needed, and Justin made me feel that way, Em. But I — I just let myself read more into it than there was."

Emily bit her lip. "I'm really sorry things didn't work out. Justin seems like a nice guy. And I'm sorry I wasn't here for you sooner — especially after you gave me so much support when I had that awful fight with Scott."

Elise took a deep breath. "How *is* Scott."

"We made up," Emily said softly. When she saw Elise's tear-streaked face brighten, her own broke out in a smile. "Do you believe he sent a letter to Candy Hearts?" She began to giggle.

"Karen saw him drop it in the submission box, only she didn't tell me. My heart almost stopped beating when I opened the letter!"

"Go on," Elise said, giving Emily's shoulder a gentle nudge. "You can't stop now. What did the letter say?"

"Elise!" Emily gasped. "Some things are *private!*"

"All right. Forget it." Elise grinned. "Just tell me where lover-boy is now?"

Emily tilted her head and began twirling her finger around a strand of hair. "He's marching to the mayor's office," she smiled, remembering her promise to meet Scott afterward at Sticky Fingers. "I wish you could have seen the size of the crowd. Just about everyone was there. It was really amazing! Jonathan had the top down on his convertible, and Justin — " She stopped abruptly and anxiously peered into Elise's eyes. "I'm sorry."

Elise sighed. "It's okay, Em. I'm not going to fall apart." She wiped her eyes with a tissue. "Just tell me why *you're* not marching?"

Emily stuffed her hands into her pockets and gave Elise a tentative smile. "I was going to — until I saw Justin. Then I figured even though we were on the outs, you might need someone to talk to."

Elise glanced at her gratefully. "I'm glad you came. I mean that." She gave Emily a quick hug. "I needed a friend right now."

Emily sighed. "Even one who's always giving advice?"

Elise thought for a moment. "Well . . . if the advice is good — "

"How about if I told you to go wash your face because we're heading over to Sticky Fingers?"

"Sticky Fingers?"

"Yep." Emily began to laugh softly. "I promised Scott I'd meet him there after the march, and I'll never be able to finish a Sundae Delight without your help." She stood up and held out her hand to Elise.

Elise broke out into a huge, happy smile. How could she resist?

Just before they got to Sticky Fingers, Elise began to have second thoughts. Why had she let Emily talk her into coming here? She didn't need the calories, and more than that, she was becoming anxious at the prospect of running into Ben — or Justin and Wendy.

Her footsteps slowed. "Em, I don't think — " she began, then stopped when a red Jeep pulled into a parking spot in front. She recognized Scott's blond hair. He spotted the girls at the same moment and stuck his head out the window.

"Hey, there! Wait for me!" he yelled.

"Scott!" Emily called out excitedly and ran over to the Jeep. As soon as Scott climbed out she gave him a quick hug. He slung an arm around her shoulder and nodded to Elise. "Glad you were able to make it."

Elise bit her lower lip and wondered if there was some way she could tactfully get out of going to Sticky Fingers. But before she could think of an excuse to return home, Scott and Emily were standing in front of the ice-cream parlor.

"Shall we go inside, ladies?" Scott asked, pushing open the thick glass doors. Instantly there was a blast of music and the sound of dozens of voices all busy chatting away.

Elise squared her shoulders and followed him inside. Most of the gang was bunched around one long table in the back. She quickly scanned their faces, but Ben's was not among them. She breathed a sigh of relief.

It's not that she didn't want to talk to him. She still considered Ben her friend. But Elise just wasn't sure he was ready to talk to her, and she didn't want to embarrass either one of them in front of their friends.

"Hey, look who's here," Jeremy quipped when he saw the three of them edging toward the table. "I was wondering if you guys were going to turn up for the celebration."

"Huh? What are we celebrating?" Emily looked at Scott.

"The fact that the mayor came out of his office and promised to have a traffic signal installed on the corner of Rose Hill Avenue and Everett Street," Scott said. "He's going to bring it up at the very next Rose Hill City Council meeting."

Emily's eyes grew wide. "You're kidding!" she blurted. "He agreed to do it?" She looked around the table.

"My guess is, as soon as he saw the marchers coming toward his office, he couldn't say 'no',"

Jonathan said, digging into his hot fudge sundae. "He's up for reelection next year, and well, need I say more?"

"The fact that we had a TV crew covering the march helped, too," Fiona added as she sipped a strawberry soda that was the same shade as her sweater.

"You forgot to mention photographers," Dee said, poking Fiona in the ribs.

Fiona giggled. "Sorry. There were also a dozen photographers and reporters marching with us. And as soon as Wendy handed the mayor our petition, he agreed the town needed a new traffic signal."

"Wow! That really does call for a celebration," Emily said, sliding into an empty chair next to Dee. Scott grabbed one from the next table, and pulling it over, straddled it with his arms folded across the back. Elise hesitated for a moment. She felt a little odd. Even though they were all her friends, would they feel awkward around her knowing about Ben and Justin?

A feeling of loss filled her heart, but she pushed it away. There was no use regretting what had happened with Justin. If she hadn't met him, she might not have realized how far apart she and Ben had grown. And that it would have been wrong for them to stay together.

So what if she hurt a little now? Falling in love wasn't always painless, and breaking up was never easy. But it was all part of growing up. The important thing was she had her friends to help her through the rough times. And as her sister, Delayne, used to say in a corny voice, "There's a lot of fish in the sea. Who knows?" Maybe someday she'd even fall in love again.

As if reading her mind, Emily leaned over to whisper in Elise's ear. "Check out that guy that just sat down at the table by the juke box." She gestured toward the front of the shop. "Tell me what you think."

Elise turned to see a great-looking boy with black hair, dark eyes and nice, broad shoulders wearing a red Kennedy High sweatshirt.

"He's gorgeous," Elise admitted. "How come I've never seen him around before?" She sneaked another peek.

"Probably because he's new to Kennedy. He just transferred from Leesburg, I'll introduce you to him if you want," she said with a twinkle in her eye.

"After we finish our Super Sundae," Elise said. "First things first, Ms. Candy Hearts."

COUPLES

Coming Soon . . .
Couples Special Edition
SEALED WITH A KISS!

"Hey," Katie said, checking her watch. "We still have a few minutes before the bell. Why don't we hang out at our old spot on the quad and see who else comes by?"

"That's a great idea, Katie," Eric agreed.

The quad was a busy place, especially in the spring and fall, and Katie and her friends were regulars there. At the start of the school year they'd taken over the "territory" originally staked by Ted, Phoebe, Chris, Woody, and Peter; who were in last year's "top" senior crowd.

As the four rounded the corner, identical frowns crossed each of their faces. Some girls, none of whom Katie recognized, and a few boys, in Stevenson jackets, had taken over their space.

"Hey, that's our cherry tree!" Katie exclaimed, tossing her red ponytail indignantly.

"And those are our benches!" Eric growled.

They looked at each other, then turned sheep-

164

ishly toward Greg and Molly. They all burst out laughing. "Listen to us!" Katie exclaimed ruefully. "You'd think we owned this place."

Katie and Molly giggled, and Eric threw his hands up in defeat. Just then the warning bell rang. "We'd better hurry," Molly said to Eric.

Katie knew she should go back to her own homeroom, but instead she lingered at the edge of the quad. One of the Stevenson girls was still sitting on what, until this morning, had been the gang's bench, and Katie couldn't help staring. The girl was flashy and beautiful. But what froze Katie in her tracks more than the girls' clothes and makeup, was her expression. She was looking around the quad like she was planning to completely take it over. Was this girl an exception, or were all the Stevenson kids like her? Katie couldn't help wondering if the school merger between Kennedy and Stevenson would really be so easy after all.

It's a Night to Remember...

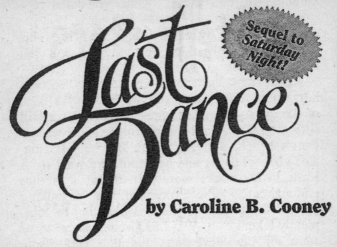

Sequel to Saturday Night!

Last Dance

by Caroline B. Cooney

Happiness and heartbreak are in the air. Eight months have passed since that special, memorable Autumn Leaves Dance. Now it's June, time for the last dance of the school year. Anne, wiser and more beautiful than ever, just wants to survive it. Beth Rose is more in love than ever...but wants Gary to fall in love with her, too. Emily, her safe world suddenly shattered, turns to Matt to make it right. Molly has been rejected, and she's out for revenge. Kip has been having the time of her life, and hopes the dance will be the perfect ending to the school year.

It will be romantic for some, heartbreaking for others...but above all, a dance the girls will never forget!

Look for it wherever you buy books!

$2.50 U.S./$3.95 CAN

Scholastic Books

LD871

They're talented.... They're winners....